To Lesley,

Love from both

Tim

T.

Alan

x

The Bunny Run

Also by Tim Topps

The Paper Caper (Matador 2013)
Too Long in the Business (Matador 2014)

TIM TOPPS

The Bunny Run

A short drive… with some diversions

Matador
9 Priory Business Park,
Wistow Road, Kibworth Beauchamp,
Leicestershire. LE8 0RX
Tel: (+44) 116 279 2299
Fax: (+44) 116 279 2277
Email: books@troubador.co.uk
Web: www.troubador.co.uk/matador

ISBN 978 1784624 408

British Library Cataloguing in Publication Data.
A catalogue record for this book is available from the British Library.

Printed and bound in the UK by TJ International, Padstow, Cornwall
Typeset by Troubador Publishing Ltd, Leicester, UK

Matador is an imprint of Troubador Publishing Ltd

FORETHOUGHT

With due humility, *"could do better"*, my Dedication is to all Teachers of English Composition, first of course in the hope of getting a few sales, but chiefly as a genuine invitation to suggest improvements – as you do.

(If this interests any educationalist among my scanty readership, details are right at the end of the book, in fact after "The End" and under the unsurprising heading "Afterthought".)

I must also, respectfully but with a lurking sense of dread, remember that distant acquaintance of Miss Dickens who terrifies us all, the immortal Emma Chiswick.

CONTENTS

I

The road to the Lone Tree

I had to get away, I just had to.

I'd not been back home more than seven minutes – not even taken off my coat and gloves on that chilly evening – but all the futile hopelessness had been building up within me for months until I now knew, all of a sudden, that my marriage was over. Not my fault though: those endless family squabbles between their family, first about their petty little disagreements and now about money. The more petty, the more they would seem to expand until they filled my head – both our heads I suppose – but I had been on the outside, just trying not to be sucked in. The origin was not even her, I suppose, basically; more, the creeping baleful influence of the rest of that awful family I had unwittingly married into... That brother...!

So I had finally drawn a line. It was finished for me. I simply called "Goodbye", shut the front door and jumped back into the car which was still ticking with engine warmth. I would drive once more along my old familiar route (twice a week for the last twenty years), which I have made into quite a historical study due to its familiarity, and which I simply called my Bunny Run.

***

Breaking off a long relationship is never easy, of course, and all the gossip pages enjoy telling us how devastated this or that celebrity is when it happens to them every eighteen months. But after a twenty-year marriage, you find your true devotion, your centre of loyalty and your source of comfort, may be entirely non-sexual, non-human… It was something I had quietly enjoyed, shared secrets with, visited regularly, always been happy to share my thoughts with in good times and bad. It was so well known to me, it would never let me down: I knew that.

I had fallen in love with a road.

***

Come with me while I tell you about it, and tell you also a few of the stories I have produced over the years. Very short, won't bore you…

I was now back in the beloved Sunbeam-Talbot that was my cocoon of joy. I relaxed within it and headed calmly into the centre of the town, past the much-loved Green Man Inn in Trumpington which was run by an old friend, Charlie Shadwell, modestly retired there after his nationwide celebrity and butt of radio jokes when he was conductor of the BBC Variety Orchestra in the days of *'ITMA'*, exchanges directed into what one imagined to be the orchestra pit from what one imagined to be the stage. How much more vivid radio can be than television.

A turning off to the left pointed to Fowlmere. I swung

away from it, purely because it was not my route; but at the same time enjoying the discomfiture of some friends who live there, when I told them that their village was not named after a lake containing wild ducks, but was actually a foul mire: a filthy marsh. I have always rather liked correcting people.

I had to drive right through the town and it was the evening rush-hour, so I tried, as so often, to switch on the car radio. It always seemed to forget it was stuck, on Radio Three, or whatever it used to be called. and had been for weeks. This means that my weekly Bunny Runs were a sort of forced induction into the sorts of music chosen for me by the wild-minded fifth-formers then running that channel. To my great fortune, that particular evening there was a Wagner concert and it was my delight to hear the *'Mastersingers'* overture and lose myself in that fantastic chord – is it in the eighth bar? – which sends a shiver through you. I'm sure this was Sullivan's one he lost.

I'm pretty good with so-called classical music, as I had a unique opportunity when I was at school during the 39-45 War. The BBC orchestras moved out into the country, and used our Hall as their main broadcasting studio for several years. We were allowed in, to listen to their rehearsals and also (if we got to know people like Adrian Boult's PA, the fearsome Mrs Beckett) to the actual broadcasts. So I'm OK on the mainstream classics.

But now, so often when I start the engine, drive off, and push the button, there is some Celtic announcer telling me inarticulately that I am about to hear an hour of ethnic chants from the backlands of Mozambique, or from the depths of Stockhausen, if they can locate it; or perhaps the output of some newly-discovered musically-inclined monk from the fourteenth century keen to echo the sainted Hildegard… Or some smart new school-leaver thinking that his own five minutes of silence is as good as that other chap's… Whoever he was. Anyway wouldn't it be? I wrote once, to say that the announcement: "In a programme note, the composer explains…" is the biggest turn-off in radio history: instant switch-off. But of course, the Radio Times didn't print it.

I came through the centre of Cambridge. There were few people about, as it was beginning to get dark and the only activity seemed to be around the pubs, and a few of the cheaper eating-places which opened early. The students would soon be noisily in Hall, and their Dons too, less noisy but infinitely more acid at their High Tables… High, I thought as I drove by, not just because of being elevated at the important end of the Hall, but because that perpetual sophisticated in-fighting over intellectual trifles and flights of fancy and non-sequiturs must be, for so many of them, the high point of their sad and cloistered little day. I wondered whether my dreadful brother-in-law might have been a less vicious and twisted person if he had received any real education: there must have been the seeds of intelligence, somewhere, and he was probably no more crooked than some of them were. But he would never have got to High Table, except perhaps to serve at it, and even then he would have stolen the spoons.

There is a strange mental stimulus that seeps into your head when you wander around age-old seats of learning.

I have experienced it in Perugia and other ancient universities on the Continent, but only in the small hours when the past seems to resurrect itself and become more real. I still get it if I walk round Oxford very early on a Sunday. You can feel an affinity with all those crazy Victorian eccentrics, whose self-indulgent bilious attacks have left their mark on history: people like Spooner, of course, but also the lesser-knowns: who was it who came down to breakfast on a pouring wet day, tapped his barometer which read 'Set Fair', and threw it out of the window saying "See for yourself, you fool !".

Down Silver Street and the punt-park over the Cam. Many of the Japanese tourists were still there, and their camera flashes were starting to illuminate the encroaching twilight gloom. When they all go home, how can they possibly bore each other with their identical snaps: me at King's… Me at the Radcliffe Camera… Me at the Tower… Me at the Globe… Me outside the Albert Hall being beaten up by survivors of the Burma Railway…

I went right along the Backs, but gave some thought to that grim old house where Frances Cornford used to live, they tell me. She was the poet so rude about the sad "fat white woman whom nobody loves" whom she saw from a train in 1910. Why do you walk through the fields in gloves, she impudently asked. One of my heroes has always been G K Chesterton, himself somewhat overweight, who replied splendidly in defence of that poor innocent obese woman in the field. "Fathead poet whom nobody reads" he wrote. Delicious – one of the best 'put-downs' in literature.

Now for the last junction, turning left opposite that large and self-important house occupied by some member of the Rothschilds who had apparently been terribly essential during the war for something-or-other we knew nothing about. Was it to do with that Cambridge Spies thing from the Thirties? Unimportant, anyway, now. I went on to the point where the official Intervarsity Run used to start, at a phone-box on the Madingley Road. This was going back to 1930s history, and it brought back memories of the Americans.

More than one pre-war undergraduate from the United States has admitted that his fondest memory of his time here is that Run, the joy of the wealthier young students in their sports cars often borrowed from an even wealthier girl-friend. The Oxford starting or finishing point was also, for obvious reasons, a telephone-box – at the top of the Banbury Road. I understand that the record for the eighty-odd miles was about that number of minutes. Many of those racers moved on very soon to Hurricanes and Spitfires or to the Flying Fortresses that followed when defence changed to attack. I wondered, as I took the road that leads towards the vast US Military Cemetery, if some of those contestants lay there now, so close to their past.

I never came near that eighty-minute target, but sometimes on a clear road I didn't do too badly. In the days before mollycoddling speed-limits, there was a stretch before Bicester where you could open up and touch a good hundred-and-ten: best at night when you could spot any side-road headlights. This was in my previous, lovely blue-

and-grey Sunbeam Talbot, which happened to be my seventh car and seven is my lucky number. She was aerodynamically superb, built like a Caravelle – that slinky French jet that went so steeply up, up and away: like a rocket and so much smoother than our own ill-fated Comets that had started to break up all over Europe so far as one heard. Smoother and sleeker too, than ours, were their professionally-alluring air-hostesses: sexily disdainful as only French girls can pretend to be, but – oh dear oh dear – those figures, and that eventual sideways look... "*...qui passez sans me voir...*"? Not always.

My route linked all the 'Bs': The main towns I would go through, are Bedford, Bletchley (well, very nearly), Buckingham and Bicester; and as I slowly learnt over the years, there are some interesting bits of history all along the Bunny Run, which in turn remind me of other little stories from time to time.

"Goodbye" was all I needed to say. No point in anything more, my life was now going to be in other directions, thanks largely to that unbearable brother-in-law. I must get on my way.

I was passing on my right the gloom of the recently-established Churchill College. That bleak concrete already starting to display the grey smear of climate which sums up the idiocy of those Sixties planners who thought that the corbusiage of the Mediterranean would look right in the teeth of the Gulf Stream's northern vicissitudes... Just as stupid as the sixteenth century architect who came back from Italy obsessed by what he had seen there, and copied it in building Houghton House – a few miles off my Run – on top of a hill and facing North. This, four hundred years before central heating; no wonder it was soon abandoned and is now a ruin.

Strange that Churchill College was at Cambridge, rather than The Other Place: after all, Winston had been born at Blenheim just outside Oxford, and buried only across the road. I suppose it was all a question of money. So was the disposal of his archive, sadly. It should have been *given* to the nation, the family keeping just copies.

An ultimate academic achievement, back in early days, must have been to contrive to have a College named after you. I suppose the fashion was set by the Scotsman, John de Baliol, around 1260, though I gather his Oxford foundation was an act of penance rather than of grandeur and beneficence: but didn't it pay off well! Talking about grandeur though: how about Isaac Wolfson? Within the space of a couple of years in the 1960s he had Colleges named after himself in both places: this hadn't been achieved since Jesus and Mary Magdalen. (Or was Wolfson doing penance too, like Baliol, for something? Should we be told?)

Oxford has always seemed a bit more maverick than the more laid-back Cambridge: and long may that last. Cambridge may be curiously proud of the rather feeble whimsy of Byron keeping a bear in his rooms in Trinity, but only Oxford would name a major College after a doorknocker.

I had now just passed that well-worn tourist

crossroads: to the right, the stately student digs of Madingley Hall, which accommodates our future Kings when the need arises to pump some intellectual knowhow into them. To the left, the road to Grantchester with its broken clock.

I'd always considered Rupert Brooke a bit of a pseud with all that hair and the brooding look, not to mention the teatime honey and self-aware upstream skinny-dipping. But then, unexpectedly, I came across his brilliant little verse *'Heaven'*, taking a look at the promise of the Next Life from the point of view of a fish: and after all, why shouldn't they have a view? If you don't know the poem, you've missed a three-minute delight. Look it up.

Over on the other, downstream side of Cambridge, is the suburb of Chesterton, the 'chester' indicating its Roman origin. However, it appears that in the case of Grantchester the name is as phoney as some of its residents: it is quite pleasant to tell them this... The late and great Editor of the Oxford Dictionary of Place-Names, Eilert Ekwall (and where the hell did *his* name come from?) traced nearly all our place-names back to the earliest documents from which he made his deductions. The River Cam in which our friend Rupert exposed himself, in homage I suppose to his equally self-indulgent Byronian predecessors, is and has always been known alternatively as Granta. Around 890 the 'Venomous Bede', as Sellar and Yeatman cruelly but delightfully mis-described our famous early historian, wrote of "the Grantan stream". The village along its banks was called 'Grantaseta' in Domesday Book and contemporary documents: not a 'chester' or 'caster' in sight. It means "the dwellers on the muddy river". So there.

Up from the crossroads we come to the resting-place of nearly 4,000 young Americans. Every time I drive past – twice a week – my thoughts go back two-thirds of a lifetime – that lifetime they never had. I am at school on a warm summer evening, lying on my back on the grass outside my boarding-house as I recover from exams that day for my Higher School Cert.: from the little time I had to glean in the newspapers, the war had begun to go well. Then, starting with a distant murmur to the west, the increasing hum and finally sky-wide drone arose; so different somehow from that intermittent throb of the German bombers we had become used to a couple of years before… As I looked up, left, and right, the sky was now packed with Flying Fortresses (and no doubt their British companions which at that height I couldn't identify, in among the horde); wave upon wave, that early evening, they passed over me with their deadly load. Retribution, I knew, for Coventry and all our other blasted cities.

But, you see, up in the dormitory we would watch the last of them depart, then revert to our secret radios tuned to Luxembourg and enjoy in the dark those entrancing Sablon and Trenet songs, somehow conveying a luxurious nostalgia even to us seventeen year olds: how was that possible? We hadn't even started our adult lives, yet the dreaminess of *'Le Bateau des Iles'*, *'J'attendrai'*, *'La Mer'* perhaps most of all (and of course as I've already mentioned, *'Vous qui passez'*) stirred inside our naive virginities some kind of latent and undiscovered eroticism... After all, even at age eight I used to be swept away by the gentle love lyrics of Astaire and Rogers. It was an odd feeling of a hidden yearning which, for many, only returned many years later – and incidentally long after my marriage, very happy though it had been for nearly 20 years. Then came those unforgettable in-house video machines along the Riviera's cafes in the 60s, which began to feature the gorgeous delight of Francoise Hardy, surely every Englishman's idea of an in-house au-pair? Remember her on that swing?

Those were our night-time dreams. Then, very early the next morning, we would be awoken by some drone, but punctuated by eccentric noises of misfunction. We would silently look out of the window at the dark shapes limping through the lightening sky, sometimes tatty and showing holes; we would see the flares being fired, whose colours told of dead or dying on board... And we would roll over and go back to sleep.

Nevertheless, much though I feel reverence for this cemetery, something about it – and indeed all such war cemeteries – bothers me.

It is the regimentation.

They line them up, thousand upon thousand, not so much memorially but geometrically. Row on row: military manipulation just as in life. The War Graves people do a wonderful job, all over the world, wherever we have been dragged in to solve other people's problems and shed our people's blood as a result: it is the cross we have to bear for having tried, beyond our strength to help people.

But don't you sometimes feel that the very mathematical precision of these burial-grounds detracts from the contemplation we need to have, for the loss of each individual, for the actual fact that they *were* individuals? Don't you sense that lining up those crosses martially, is somehow belittling? I once came across a truly 'abandoned' graveyard somewhere up north, it might have been in Hull, where I derived from its mossy, crumbling, leaning tombstones a much deeper feeling of mortality and our ultimate mysteries, than I could ever get from an 'on parade' regiment of the immortal dead, all lined up and ready for inspection with the RSM heavy-breathing right behind them...

There was a special Armistice Day service in 1936 when I lived in Nairobi. I watched from my father's office opposite the War Memorial, as he laid his official wreath. I was impressed by the way that blacks, whites and Asians (who ran nearly all the shops) came together to pay their respects on this mutually shared occasion: that 'sharing' being later commented upon as a desirable Scouting aim in a letter to my father from his close friend Baden-Powell. But on that particular day of Remembrance, while I was proud to have helped my mother and her British Legion friends in making the poppies, a little incident later disturbed me, greatly: even at that age.

The storm-blasted, leaning Lone Tree was out on the Athi plains, some miles from Nairobi, and people used to go there for picnics. It wasn't far from a modest little Army cemetery taking one back to 1914-18, and though we went there later that Armistice Day, I wrote my story many years later. I reckon the best thing is probably the title, given the circumstances.

LONE TREE

It wasn't a particularly far-flung corner of the Empire: East Africa was fairly well-known and accessible in the 1930s, or at any rate the large towns. You could get to Nairobi by Imperial Airways in their great lumbering biplanes, or more likely make a proper holiday of it and take the Union Castle boat that sailed out with such clockwork regularity: "Every Friday at 4 o'clock," wasn't it, they used to advertise? A splendid business trip for visiting VIPs, out through Suez, buying your topee at Simon Artz emporium as you passed Egypt; then back round the Cape, and all on the tax-payer or the share-holder. There was no shortage of volunteers from Home, to attend any special celebration in Nairobi, unless of course it happened to be the rainy season…

With all that eager talent available, there were only a few residual and more domestic occasions in the year when my father was called upon to add his weight, and get dolled up in his slightly-less-than-splendid white Dress Uniform with the row of medals and his white hat with the feathers on top. Nowhere near so imposing as some of the greater dignitaries like the Governor of the Colony, or even the Chief of Police; but it was enough at the time for me to feel the reflected warmth of a minor glory, whenever he put it all on. This helped a good deal when you were nine and so many other people seemed to be ten or eleven...

One of those occasions was Armistice Day. In our present hardbitten world, that is a commemoration largely gone out of fashion. True, we still go through the motions in an automatic sort of way, but from the time we dropped the actual day November the Eleventh, and shifted our remembrance to "the nearest Sunday" because it was more convenient, it was evident that we were trying to disguise the awful fact that we have lost interest.

Back in 1936 though, you were only 18 years away from the day of the Armistice itself: everyone's parents had been personally involved. You could, as it were, still smell the mud. What was more, in a community like Kenya the ceremony took on an extra significance which I now suppose was rather ahead of its time. As we stood in my father's office at eleven that morning, looking down upon the War Memorial where he was waiting to lay his official wreath with the others, I can clearly remember how I was struck by the significance of the extraordinary mixture of people taking part. It was not the row of shining decorated big-wigs, the local representatives of a dozen or so countries of Europe, perhaps America, and the various Dominions around the Empire... Nor, even, was it the magnificence of the Band of the K.A.R. – the King's African Rifles – who were poised nearby in a glory of silver and brass and leopard-skins, with the rest of their parade stretching away down the Avenue in a double line of spruce khaki drill, every one topped off by a red fez: that was stirring, but not *moving*. No, the thing that got through to me on that day, and does still, was the strange "togetherness" of the common crowd. Behind that line of askaris, standing in absolute silence as the distant gun fired, were black men, white men, yellow and brown men... in their best suits, or grubby shorts, brilliant expensive saris, loin-cloths, Sunday garden-party hats, or second-hand pyjamas exposing bare feet... The whole confection spread out across the centre of Nairobi like licorice-allsorts over a table-top.

The bandsmen suddenly rustled as though a breeze had blown through them, and a moment later "O God our help in ages past" rose up past our window in a massive bewilderment of different accents. I was following the words on my programme, along with the English and the Germans down there, the Africans, the Boers, Indians, Arabs... "Time, like an ever-rolling stream..." All her sons: and there they all were, who – not so many years ago – had been at each other's throats. I sang away like mad.

This was the first time I had actually taken part in the preparations. My mother had taken me along to the British Legion a few days earlier, to help her – with many others – make the wreaths and button-hole poppies from supplies which had been shipped out from England: they were artificial flowers of course, but we had real shiny leaves to add to them. I had produced some pretty dreadful specimens, clumsy-fingered as ever, and no doubt one of the kind ladies dismantled my wreaths after I had gone home and re-made them according to the textbook. However, with my individual poppies I was quite competent, and we had taken a small box of them away with us because it had become a tradition in Nairobi in recent years, to go to the old Military Cemetery outside the town on the edge of the Plains, and place a poppy on every grave.

So in the afternoon when we had changed out of our best clothes, we drove off, making an excursion of it since all the schools closed for the day; and alongside the poppies, with me on the back seat, was the far more interesting hamper containing our picnic.

Almost anywhere on the dusty Plains in those days, you could stop the car with the whole landscape to yourselves, and the grazing herds would amble past… We drew up by a single scrawny thorn-tree, flat-topped and tattered by generations of giraffe, which leaned out at the roadside with nothing but scrub for miles around. This was "Lone Tree", a famous local land-mark which for many years epitomised the Kenya countryside in guide-books and souvenir water-colours… As a tree, it wasn't much to write Home about; but as a symbol of Life on the Plains, and as a notable meeting-place at night both for lions and for lovers, it was in the history books.

We demolished our picnic, and played some cricket, and then in the late afternoon we continued to the remote cemetery with its rows of crosses and headstones, each with a name, rank and regiment in meticulous letters…

Many families used to join in this simple little pilgrimage, and most of the graves already had a poppy at their head: we were probably the last to arrive. My parents walked along between the rows, and I followed reading some of the names – in case there were any from families I knew at school, I suppose; though indeed most of the dead, sent from Home to be killed in the German East Africa campaign of 1915, had had no plans whatever to settle here, let alone die in its defence.

We had disposed of all our poppies now, and were heading back to the car with the empty box, in something of a hurry because my parents had to attend a function that night. As I ran after them, something caught my eye. I stopped in my tracks.

Right in the corner of the Cemetery, past the end of the final row, and with no poppy at all, was a pathetic little cross of black wood. It was so hidden by weeds, you could scarcely see it, leaning askew, untended, with the name illegible on its cross-piece. I went up close and peered at it, but no, it was impossible to read.

I called to my father urgently, but he was looking at his watch and beckoning me to the open door of the car. Quickly I looked around but there was no spare poppy on any nearby grave, and to deprive one of the others would be unfair…

The whole way home I thought silently about this, and the sad loneliness of the unnamed and un-remembered grave got worse and worse. On its own, for the rest of the year, that was bad enough: but to have no poppy…! All the emotion of the day was building up inside me, though I sensed that it would be stupid to let it out in public: the grown-ups, after all, had their own lost relatives to remember. To this unknown soldier the respects had to be my own.

While my parents were getting ready for their evening appointment at Government House, I went to see my best friend Jan, who lived down the road. To him I poured out my feelings, and as usual, he understood at once: of course the little wooden cross should have a poppy, the finest we could produce. He got as worked up as I was, and we would both have been weeping about it by then if we hadn't been so excited making plans...

Jan came back with me for an early supper; and then the grown-ups went off in the car, and under the benevolent and guileless eye of the house-boy Kitau, we were on our own. Jan kept him talking in the kitchen while I slipped out into the hall and dialled the number of Ranji our usual Indian taxi-man, who knew my voice well enough from the frequent times he had run me to or from the school, with which he had a mysterious special relationship... There was always a motor-car crisis at our house: radiators boiled and batteries went flat as often as not, when my mother got into a driving-seat. I even remember the car number: T.1665. "Plague year", my father said grimly when he first saw it.

Ranji assumed I was ringing on behalf of my parents and promised to be right along. We told Kitau we would both be at Jan's house till my bedtime, and I would see him then. I took a huge floppy basket called a *kikapu*, which my mother used to have filled with fresh vegetables at the covered market for a shilling a time; and we marched out of the house, purposefully in the direction of Jan's, then doubled back on our tracks to the front gate, there to await Ranji in his peeling silver Chevrolet. Kitau, suspecting nothing, was busy at the cooker making his supper, a mash-up of mealies they called *posho*, and very good too.

"Where's the bwana?" asked Ranji, and we told him that *we* were the bwanas tonight, so down town please and step on it.

He looked around for my mother. "Come on Ranji," we said, "I bet this useless old tincan won't even *reach* the centre of town. Or have your headlights fallen off?" We also threatened that there had been many criticisms of his vehicle recently, and my father's friend the Chief of Police had asked me my opinion, whether a much more up-to-date taxi firm ought not to have the school contract...

We were down town surprisingly soon. We instructed the muttering Ranji to keep his engine running and his lights off, and out into the gloom we crept with our big kikapu...

A lot of scrambling in the darkness, and a couple of minutes later, we were back. Ranji's eyes opened wider than they had been for thirty years.

"Does your father know," he gasped, "what it is that you are going to be doing?"

"This is official business, Ranji – just drive on."

"Drive on, drive on... Yes yes, I will drive on – straight home I will drive on."

Jan said to me casually: "The Blantyre Garage have brand-new Packards, have you seen?"

I nodded. "And they don't charge waiting time."

Ranji hit himself twice on the forehead, then sighed deeply and switched off the engine. He turned round to us in the back. "You boys now – you are going to be getting me arrested – what is it, what is it that you have got inside that kikapu?"

So in the end we told him. And he, an old soldier

himself with a display of grubby medal-ribbons and with old Army photos, stuck in his driving-mirror, took us straight out to the Military Cemetery without a word of further argument, came in with us while we took the Governor' s enormous wreath which we had stolen from the Cenotaph, stood to attention as we laid it on the sad little grave, and sped us home again in silence.

When we got out of the taxi he looked at us man to man, as one of a team that has done a good job. He quite refused to make any charge because, as he said, "It was an event of importance".

I walked in past Kitau who was still stirring his posho. The wireless was broadcasting a repeat of the Armistice Day ceremony. "Time like an ever-rolling stream bears all her sons away," everybody was singing... "They fly forgotten, as a dream dies at the opening day..."

Not forgotten, I said to myself proudly, as I went upstairs to bed.

II

The road to Lloyd George

People today tell me that they have never heard of the Lone Tree, though I have old Christmas cards of it: I suppose it eventually just fell over – a scratching giraffe would easily have done it – and then rotted away like so much of the old pre-war Kenya where everybody seemed to be happy, apart from those unspeakable wastrels who were ruining all our good intentions by their mindless behaviour, far from the plodding rest of us, in the sardonically-named Happy Valley. Some time after those fools had ruined it all, I imagine the remains of the old tree had been bulldozed away like so many other of the vindictive demolitions that came with the optimistically-named 'independence'...

That clumsy little wooden cross has probably gone, too. In real life, no other boy and no taxi-driver or giant Governmental wreath was involved: we got home, I wept, we drove back, I laid a few poppies, all privately within the family. But, you see, the memory has stayed with me all these years.

I would imagine that most writers of short stories will agree that many of their inspirations come from an insignificant idea, sown in the corner of the brain and then unexpectantly watered by an event which at first sight seems completely unrelated. It may still lie dormant for years until a sideways shaft of light reveals it as a completely obvious story. I've never asked any of them (I don't *know* any of them) but I bet they often think of the last page first. Look at the last lines of O. Henry or Saki...

Then there is the other kind of short story which developed in the last century, where nothing much happens but we are supposed to know the characters – or at least one of them – far better at the end. This is a prose version of some of Robert Browning's stuff; it must be very easy to write it badly. But I don't know about you – I don't like being left 'up in the air' at the end of twenty minutes' hard concentration (which it always is).

Those 'slices of life', as their authors like to call their spotless character-studies, usually serve to make me more convinced than ever that we humans are ill-equipped to handle life's minimal problems. Ever since the cave-dwelling days, we have learnt to tackle the major worries of our existence: when times were bad and our winter survival was under threat, we hunted more fiercely, took more risks over it, stayed out later, while the womenfolk gathered further and got more scratched, no doubt, on the brambles and thorns. At night we would draw pictures of animals on the walls to entertain and distract our starving youngsters...

But while we have been programmed to put up with the big discomforts of essential hardship, the lesser ones get on our nerves, get through to us. They wriggle subtly under our skin, like the jiggers in Africa, laying their eggs inside our subconscious, waiting to hurt and itch when the opportunity comes along. Consider: a man can get his leg blown away quite calmly ("By God, Sir, so you have" at Waterloo); but he can moan for months about a barking dog, or his wife for days about a broken fingernail. Does something inside us enjoy getting angry at things which – we know – hardly matter a damn, purely because we *know* they are insignificant and no real harm lies there? An escape, then, from hard realities?

One of the oldest and best forms of escape from our realities, of course, is fiction; but when we settle down to wade through almost any of The World's Greatest, we – or I anyway – face suffocation by a great heavy book with close print going on for ever. Anything by our famous novelists I find utterly off-putting the moment I start. There just isn't the time... and if I do persevere (that sounds like a hero from a Restoration comedy: Sir Percy Vere?); if I do that, the plot is usually so involved and some of the characters so anguished, the volume gets heavier and heavier, and I can scarcely find the energy to crawl across to the life-raft of the TV... ("What date does this have to be back at the Library? Not until then??")

In these days of endless television and limited concentration-span, books need to be short – or at the very least, chapters do, and within them, the sentences. The most sensible writers saw the trend coming, a long time ago. I'll cite only two. Oscar Wilde was spot-on, and far ahead of his time, with his dry comments on the death of Little Nell... And closer to us but not very, much-admired and much-maligned AA Milne produced in the two Pooh books something very clever indeed.

My hypothesis is this: Milne was not writing for children at all. Well, obviously, stories for them to enjoy; but underneath, there are little mischievous asides that will go right over their heads, and these make the books immortal. So many adults, especially the childless or those who left night-time story-reading to somebody else, have missed out. They should read or read again: they will find the chapters, the sentences, even the words quite short, and the whole thing manageable!

I was eight, and in a nursing-home delirious with a mixture of malaria and blood-poisoning, plus the suspicion of something stuck in my gall-bladder – God, how we suffered for the Empire – when they gave me the two Pooh books... This, it turned out, was rather a mistake: in my lucid intervals I read long into the night, and my laughter was so uncontrollable that the staff moved me into a private room so the rest of the inmates could get some sleep. Needless to say, as soon as I had dozed off, Matron took away the books and could herself, they told me, be heard down the corridor in hysterics.

Among my readers, if any, there will be some who doubt all this; but then, look at some of the characters. Admittedly, Christopher Robin comes across as a bit of a goody-goody (and suffered dreadfully from that entirely non-Pooh verse about saying his prayers; big mistake and let's dismiss it at once, follow him headlong downstairs and move on to the books, shall we?). It is his friends in the Forest who are interesting, and clearly aimed at an adult reader... Always remember that the story is being read, usually, by a parent sitting on the edge of the night-time bed. The laughter is going to be two-edged...

First of all, let's take Eeyore. He is everybody's antisocial (though he tries) maiden aunt, for whom all is terrible-and-sad, though we are pretty sure he revels in that sadness. Then, Piglet: everyone's timid underdog: "Hello Piglet, this is Tigger, he has just come to the Forest". Piglet moved round the table: "When is he going?". These are grown-up caricatures, of whom young kids will have had no experience.

Supremely though, we adults can surely identify with the sequence where the fussy Rabbit – obviously that petty man from the Council with his pension-guaranteed bossiness and his habit of writing instructional letters to the other denizens, then taking them round to read aloud in case the recipients are illiterate, as mostly they are – visits the quasi-educated Owl (who can proudly sign his name 'Wol') in his home in the upper branches. Rabbit starts to read his pompous message...

"Owl looked at Rabbit and wondered whether to push him off the tree". Now, I submit: that has to be an adult joke, and incidentally timeless. You don't put that sort of thing into a 1920s book purely for children.

I mentioned Eeyore. His depressive character is something that most youngsters would never have come across or personally had to deal with. Querulent oldies were a problem for one's parents. If old Uncle Carruthers, back at last from India, had gone Doolali, or if Grandma was hearing voices, Mum and Dad would deal with it. Nothing about Eeyore would affect the youngsters at all. I had an Eeyorish aunt: as a passenger in the rear seat of my father's Morris Oxford, early Fifties, we stalled on the rocking crest of a small hump-backed bridge along a remote minor road, hoping to locate some ruin or other. As we perched there and Dad revved uselessly, Doris leaned forward and read aloud, as she was wont to do, the wording on the faded and leaning notice-board: "This bridge," she said very clearly, "is unfit for motor traffic."

But the old girl lived on, cooking and cleaning alone in her flat, to the splendid age of 102 – and only died then because she tripped in the kitchen and her fridge fell on her. When I visited her in hospital in Eastbourne the day she died, she joked about it, because she could see the funny side. (Now *she* used to enjoy the Pooh books, even without children). She then said: "I think perhaps it's time to go."

RIP, Doris old dear, who used to take me to West End musicals during the War – *Merry Widow*, *Floradora*, *Count of Luxembourg* – when I was home from school. She had never married, and the family always saw her as a – rather ugly – old maid... But when I went through her sparse belongings I found, wrapped carefully in an envelope, a gleaming gold half-sovereign dated 1914. There was no message, just the coin, and its date on the envelope in ink and in a handwriting not hers... Now, *there's* a story.

* * *

It occurred to me at this point as I drove along the rather boring stretch of road that leads up to the evocative Caxton Gibbet: I had never asked my frightful brother-in-law if he had read the Pooh books. Pretty unlikely. Then I remembered, he'd probably stolen them from his mother. I wonder whether thieves take the time to read or otherwise enjoy the things they steal? He would have had plenty of time for reading when he was inside the last two or three times, they've cut out hard labour and it's much more like a well-regimented health farm, so you come out after your three years' of free Board-and-Lodgings full of energy to start over again, making use, obviously, of all the inside networking you've been doing... What a farce.

How could a man like him ever understand – he'd laugh at me, indeed he had, come to think of it – if I confessed to him – as I have done on occasions to more understanding and sensitive friends, and am now also confiding in you – that I can never read the final chapter of *'The House At Pooh Corner'* without crying...?

Of course it is just a matter of *Temps perdu*, I fully realise that. But also, a seam of compassion different from nostalgia, which can equally run through the unhardened veins of the young. I don't suppose for a moment that any youngster would understand my distress at the end of that book. But how about this: when I had a young family, we used to enjoy a paperback of jokes by I-forget-which great cartoonist, many reprinted from Punch in the days when it was still clever and amusing. My boys found them all very funny, right up to the last page, which was a drawing of Noah's Ark sailing away as the waters rose. On the shore behind it, having arrived too late, were two lovely unicorns. My young son, who couldn't have been more than five, was so distressed that he tore the page out.

People are so different. When I recounted this touching incident to my parents, a little hesitantly, I noticed this disparity for the first time. My father was moved by the story and quite moist-eyed, as he had been by the end of Pooh when I spoke of it; my mother shuddered at my mawkishness. Somebody must have told her once, probably back in the Twenties when it was all the rage, that she was "a tough cookie", and she had always felt thereafter that she had to live up to it. I wonder whether, in her 30s in Government service in Nairobi, she had perhaps hankered after the artificial excitements echoing down from Happy Valley to her ex-officio but boring membership of the Muthaiga Club? She did, after all, work as a secretary in Erroll's office...

I also remembered the day when, in 1938, they had to leave me at boarding-school in England before returning to Kenya (and would not then see me for seven years – whyever is seven my lucky number??). It had been my father who carried my bags into the changing-rooms, while Mum stayed in the car...

All quite different, though, after they had retired, and then after Dad died. Sometimes, as they grow old, people's minds and attitudes strangely re-develop, don't they? After Dad's stroke in his mid-seventies, he slowly "went off": I'll long remember his doctor's brutal – to naïve me – words: "He's dementing". That may be true, and perfectly intelligible to a medic., but to a simple man in the street, the sudden word is harsh.

My mother, however, once settled into a comfortable care-home widowhood, became a different person. One felt she was happily relaxing after forty years of "showing the flag" and producing the drinks and canapés in all corners of the Empire. In fact, it was retirement for her and for that Empire, both.

She developed a quite acute sense of the ridiculous, too; and this little story, though it never happened, might well have done.

LLOYD GEORGE KNEW MY MOTHER, ANYWAY

"Mind you," said my mother, "I was interfered with once, when I was about six."

"You'd better not mention that in here," I told her. "The old girls will all be saying – she's eighty-eight now and still talking about it!"

"…It was in a cemetery in Islington."

"Who was the man?" I asked.

"Eh?"

"Who was – Turn up your hearing-aid."

"Wait a minute, I'll turn up my hearing-aid." It whistled as I shouted my question again. "I don't know who he was." She thought for a moment. "He wasn't a Methodist – not one of ours, anyway… Might have been a Wesleyan."

"He wasn't Reformed, that's for sure," I joked.

"But they took me to the Doctors and they said I was all right so nobody bothered any more... Mrs. Ridley had to go to the Doctors yesterday."

"Surely no-one's been – "

"...With her eyes. She had to go with her eyes. You always drive too fast, Alan."

I had to think about that: "Would I be right in saying that Mrs. Ridley's son took her for a drive with the car window down, and she got a draught in her eye?"

"What are you talking about, Mrs. Ridley doesn't have a son. Who told you that?"

"I thought – "

"*Just* like your father, always driving too fast."

I couldn't let that one go. "Now listen, Mum, you know jolly well the fastest Dad ever went was in the hearse to his own funeral – he didn't believe human life could survive over 45 miles an hour."

"*He* ought to have been a Meals-on-Wheels man."

"A what!"

"...Better than that one who drove poor Mrs. Ridley too fast to the hospital when she got the pepper in her eye yesterday. Drink your tea while it's hot."

I felt suddenly that we had achieved something, and sat exhausted with my teacup while she flipped the pages of her newspaper. She sniffed at a couple of photographs, and then went back to the original subject.

"All this sex and drugs and music," she muttered, "and all mixed in on the same pages with pictures of the Royal Children. It didn't happen when I was young, everyone going off with everyone... When I was a girl we had, well, standards. You didn't just... Especially when you were married… I don't know," she said, and she shook her head and put the paper down.

I looked around the little room which had been her home for ten years now; the familiar pictures on the walls, rescued from the house sale only because they were the smallest ones and would fit in; the old yellow photos in frames almost completely hidden by more recent snapshots stuck all the way round and curling at the edges. And the array of today's birthday cards, still making a proud show, but noticeably fewer less than last year's and fewer again than the year before.

"Mind you," she began again suddenly, "I had my moments."

It was time for her evening Scotch and water, and I got up and crossed the bed-sitter to pour her a large one. It's not every day you're eighty-eight.

"You'll get me talking," she said as she took a sip; and then: "Isn't there too much water in this? Mrs. Bloom across the hall – she's the refugee lady – she told me she saw Miss Wetherell come in when it was nearly dark, carrying *two* bottles of gin. Two! She's the one who likes to play Scrabble but you have to let her win, otherwise she cries."

"It's worth it," I said, "if you get a gin every time."

"You drink too much," said my mother scoldingly over her glass. She picked up part of her newspaper again. "I don't know what the Government is doing; my pension's gone down this month and the Tax on it's gone up."

I sighed. "You've got it wrong again. I explained it to you last week…" But her hearing-aid had gone off. "Is it the battery?" I asked.

"No," she corrected me, "it's the battery." She fiddled with it until it began to whistle.

"Mrs. Lever's always talking about Peru," she told me. I expressed interest in this, cautiously. "*Her* hearing-aid comes from some special people and they send a man to service it."

"Not from Peru?"

"Do you really think so? Anyway, I saw an advert in the paper and filled it in but then I think I threw the paper away, so that's all right. Drink your tea while it's hot." She looked across at her cards. "It's quite nice being eighty-eight, I feel as if I've reached a sort of target."

I did some calculations. "I reckon you must be almost the oldest inhabitant."

She visibly preened herself: "Well, apart from Mrs. Wheeler-Webster who you can't count really. All our married life I've taken good care of *my* appearance, you know that."

I was dying to know why poor Mrs. Wheeler-Webster didn't count, but she went on: "Oh yes, I've had my moments; but I was never unfaithful to you really, not after Alan was born."

"*I'm* Alan," I said.

"Oh, silly me – I keep getting you muddled up with your father, now your hair's going grey. You ought to put on that Roman stuff... But I did once, you know, sort of..."

"What, be unfaithful to Dad?"

"It was when we were engaged, I went out to Germany after the War to see him, I suppose it was about 1920, it was the time I met Lloyd George."

"You met Lloyd George!"

"Well, I didn't really *meet* him, but he was on the boat and bumped into me coming round a corner... Such lovely eyes." She went a bit dreamy... "Miss Dixon across the corridor's got lovely eyes too, you'd never guess she was blind."

"Tell me about Lloyd George – did he speak to you?"

"Ooh yes. He said Sorry, and patted my shoulder. It was ever so exciting – I was only about twenty."

"That's not being unfaithful."

"You are silly – it wasn't *him*. It was a young German. We met in a cafe one day."

"Where was Dad?"

"Well," she said, "I don't know why I'm telling you this. He was over there in the British Army of Occupation, on the Rhine, and he had to be away in camp most of the time. I wasn't really supposed to be there. It didn't matter him being away, not all that much, because we weren't... well, people didn't in those days, not like – " and she rustled the daily paper fiercely as if to shake off the unsavoury news-items.

Then she confided: "Mrs. Bloom – she's the refugee lady you know – always has the Financial Times. It's *pink*. I thought it was about horse-racing. They were watching racing on the television yesterday up in the main lounge, but I don't want sit up there with that crowd of old women."

"Get back to Germany," I said.

"No," she replied in a puzzled tone, "I don't think so."

"What?"

"What?" She tutted. "*Do* listen. I said I don't think so. I don't think Mrs. Bloom is going back to Germany. She's been here since 1937." She peered at her glass. "There's *far* too much water in this."

I got up again and did the decent thing with the whisky bottle.

"*He* never touched a drop," my mother said admiringly, and after a minute I realized we were back on course. "Rudi was such a quiet man. We simply sat in the cafe and he talked and talked...

"I met him every morning," she went on as if I was being let into the conspiracy. "Rudi really fell for me... Or was his name Jodi, I don't always remember everything any more... No, it was Rudi... But anyway, I wouldn't do anything about it because of your father. I just stayed in the pension-hotel-thing and saw Dad when he could get away, and the rest of the time I was with Addi... Rudi... What *was* it?"

"You old flirt!" I said. "Was he handsome?"

"No, not really, not at all what you'd call handsome; but great personality, and so keen, so full of ideas. He was bursting with ideas, like a dynamo buzzing away with them. All the things he was going to do... Though mind you, my German was a bit rusty and I truly didn't understand all he was on about...

"He used to sit holding my hand..." She thought for a while. "Rudi said... Addi said. Oh dear this whisky *is* making me talk... He said he would give it all up, all his ambitions and plans, just to marry me. He just sat there and said so, and he had tears in his eyes... I don't think he'd had a lot to do with girls. I think he was shy and of course he'd been in the War and all that."

"What happened?" This was a story I'd never heard before, though my mother had always enjoyed telling us her adventures.

"Nothing much," she said quickly. Then she glanced at me roguishly and I could see what young men had liked in her. "Would I tell you if it had? And how do you know I'm not making it up anyway?"

"Well?"

"I never told your father. I've never told anybody... You shouldn't give me these drinks." She shrugged. "I went back to England, Dad and I got married, very soon you came along, and so – you know – life goes on, doesn't it? But I sometimes wonder..."

"Why don't you try to trace him now?" I asked. "Do you know his other name?"

"He was just Rudi... No, wait a minute," she scratched her nose, "That wasn't it... Addi. Just imagine, I simply can't remember. I'm getting as bad as Mrs... Mrs. – er – Mrs. Upstairs. Oh well, I had to make a clean break, so it's probably a good thing I've never remembered, things had gone too far."

I didn't like the sound of that, but there was more coming up fast.

"Mind you," she considered for a moment, "he may well have turned out a bit unreliable. Not like your Dad – and not a bit like Lloyd George, either. No. He had rather small eyes, and they were a bit close together – "

I laughed at that. "Oh, well, that's nothing – people say that about me, too."

She looked at me thoughtfully, for rather too long... "Yes," she said, "they do, don't they?"

She drained her glass and got up. "Jodi..." she

pondered. "Rudi... Rudolf..." Her face lit up. "Ah, Adolf, that was it. He was Adolf Something-or-Other. I think he was going into local government if I wouldn't marry him. So full of ideas... And that little moustache..."

"Well my dear, I must toddle along, I'm having supper with that nice Mrs. Bloom, she's the refugee lady, you know..." And off she went down the long antiseptic corridor. It was the last time I saw my old mother.

It can't be very often that a mother tells her son that his real father was Hitler. The trouble is, I shall never know the truth now: as she went round the corner, her hearing-aid was whistling so loud I couldn't tell whether she was laughing or not.

III

The Road to Status

But, yes, mothers can be a problem. Inevitably I thought of the chaos that had just been caused at home by the silly wording of my wife's mother's will: her children were now at each others' throats, shouting across the table, even in public, which I could never understand... The old lady had left nearly everything to her daughter, cutting off her brother because of his various troubles with the police. I tried to keep out of it all, but you know how it is...

Strangely though, she had been quite a quiet and pleasant old thing – I never knew her husband so I can't identify where that brother got his awfulness from; I really didn't want to know, I just had to get away from it all for good – and now, of course I had done. He certainly hadn't inherited her sense of humour, either: I remember she had really enjoyed the Pooh books I had lent her, though, mind you, I never got them back. She maintained she had asked her son to return them, but my guess is that they ended up at that stall in Cambridge market, and they were quite scarce early editions, too, late Twenties. The wretched man must have flogged them for drugs when he was between prison stretches, strumming that bloody guitar... No more of that, either!

⋆⋆⋆

I had come to the end of a boring few miles of dispiriting rural bungalows whose occupants presumably survived by buying each others' eggs; and now there was the bleak Caxton Gibbet crossroads. Here I crossed, vertical on the map, the original Great North Road, with its shades of headless highwaymen and galloping Miss Margaret Lockwood, swinging between James Mason and Stewart Granger in exciting black-and-white. Why is mono so much more evocative than Technicolour? Even in a hopelessly over-the-top film about Hollywood's extravagances like – say – 'Sunset Boulevard', the plush furnishings, the drapes, the costumes are all the more acceptable for being left completely to our own imaginations. I suppose that when it's all spelt out to us in full colour, it is a great temptation to be distracted from the plot and sit there thinking: "That purple's wrong" or "Whoever thought those greens would go together?" or "Where did he get that tan, up there in the Arctic?". With b-&-w you are happily on your own.

Nowadays, I think our imaginations are under-exercised. It's all laid out for us, like some stranger choosing our books and clothes. There must be a whole generation of younger cinema-goers, even TV viewers as well, who lack much of the ability, the experience, to 'see' a picture for themselves in its colours, unless they have actually had the colours exposed to them. In 1964 in Paris, Jacques Tati staged an invited opening night at a remote Left Bank cinema for the re-launch of *'Jour de*

Fete', which he had retouched with little areas and spots of colour here and there. It was an interesting though very minor experiment. By accident I was there: it's nice to have shaken his hand. But I can't say the basic attraction of that delightful film was much enhanced: the dabs of colour amid the basic black and white were rather a distraction and took one's eye off his visual jokes. I don't think he repeated the experiment although his later films went into full colour. They weren't so good, were they?

To tinker with an existing film is nearly as futile as, in nearly every instance, to re-make it. Can you imagine Laurel and Hardy 'improved' by colour? And how about *Casablanca*: surely that last "beautiful friendship" scene must stay as it is?

And yet, look at cartoons. Here the opposite seems to apply. Tom and Jerry are a delight, colour helps enormously; and the early Disney and Felix efforts seem feeble, largely for lack of colour... Snow White and Bambi and Fantasia would be unthinkable... It's all too difficult, I told myself as I drove past the gibbet, which stood there black against a twilight sky.

Down the old highway to my left was the little village of Caxton, where in happier times we had very nearly bought an old Georgian house, an ex-pub with a Victorian postbox in its wall, and a green pond out the back, which must have held three hundred years of urinations, but which I still craved to dredge and perhaps find loads of valuable old discarded bottles.

I spent a lot of time thinking – I nearly said 'pondering'

– about discarded bottles. Just across from Caxton was the somewhat decadent Wimpole Hall, quietly decaying in those days after years of US Army occupation… Think back over a century or two before the days of bossy local councils, and the infestation of Health & Safety: where would those Victorians and their forebears have dumped their rubbish? Obviously, they just dug a hole at the far reaches of the estate and chucked everything in; and we know there are now enterprising people who locate some of these places, and we see their cleaned-up retrievals in every antiques market. Will anyone, some day soon, set up in business to get this organised nationally, sharing fifty-fifty with each Stately Home owner: no doubt a load of rubbish, but equally some nice onion-shaped wine bottles. At Wimpole they will no doubt have to dig first through a layer of Jack Daniels.

Even more exciting, and surely rewarding, would be to form an organisation with the sole purpose of exploring deeply down old wells. There must be an enormous trove at the bottom of village, farm and manorhouse wells, let alone those at important mansions. They will have been created hundreds of years ago, (just imagine the effort!), and used daily for centuries: a huge variety of containers must have been dropped down by drunken coachmen or by housemaids having amorous distractions. I even went so far, years ago, as to design a van fully equipped with suitable ropes and pulleys, to lower the researcher down, and crank up finds; there was a metal umbrella attached, to save him from falling bricks… I wrote to a paper about this brilliant idea but they didn't print it…

* * *

Wimpole, now – wherever did that name come from? Way back in 1087 in Domesday it is 'Winepola', but Mr Ekwall sensibly shies away from the temptation that it had to do with supports for a vineyard, because nothing is that easy. No, it was Wina's pool whoever Wina was; and what if his pool had been that pond behind the pub?

It is intriguingly impossible to know how words were said, in days gone by. Was he Wina to rhyme with 'cleaner', or with 'finer'? But then, in several languages the 'w' comes out as 'v'… One debates these inconsequential things all the time when driving alone.

For a long time, I confess, I must have made a great fool of myself by mispronunciations which went uncorrected, I suppose because listeners were too polite to put me right (or maybe, at school, too much enjoying the spectacle). With a shudder now, I remember saying 'epitome' to rhyme with 'home'; I used to pronounce 'awry' to rhyme with 'story', despite more than one reading of Omar Khayyam (I must have been skipping), where "They sneer at me for reading all awry" would have put right anybody more attentive, and what an appropriate quotation, come to think of it. Once, talking to the English master, and referring to Barrie's 'The Admirable Crichton', I mis-said everything except 'The' – thank you, Mr Benn, for quietly correcting me beyond the hearing of the class. I have a slight weakness for correcting people, and I hope I would have been equally considerate…

Place-names themselves can be tricky, of course, and

we all must have delighted in foreigners trying to cope with Worcester or Warwick, let alone Beaulieu and Wemyss. In past times, dipping again into Mr Ekwall, the documents can show an enormous variation in the spelling – and hence the locals' pronunciation – of even quite simple names. Take the village of Girton, which I would have passed twenty-five minutes ago. Few places could be more straightforward: "a settlement on gravelly soil", (or 'grit'). Indeed, it was written as 'Gretton' or 'Gryttune' before the Conquest, and 'Gretone' in Domesday. Somewhere along the line, the locals elided the 'r' so that it slid towards the '-ton' and was lazier and easier to say with a straw (later, your clay pipe) in your mouth. Try saying 'griton' aloud and you can hear the county accent. And anyway, you very seldom had to say it at all: you never went anywhere beyond the nearest market and everybody knew where you came from. Travelling merchants would need to know your village's name but never had need to spell it, nor – probably – the ability… Your priest could write it, when he had to; but apart from him, the record-keepers were only the tax collector and the scribes needing to confirm parish boundaries and land transactions. They would write place-names down as they heard them, and that is what varied over the centuries.

In researching local history one needs to remember how few country people could read or write until quite modern times. I often think how silly the axe-grinding Nationalists are in Wales or Ireland in their insistence upon their road signs including their message in the dying local language: surely these days, the few people able to speak only Gaelic can't read it anyway? It would be interesting to work out the cost of all that wasted signwriting, divided by the number of only-Gaelic-speakers, to establish how much per person the cost of the pointless exercise has been (and how much per the rest of us, paying for it).

When I was running an insurance business for students, the Union President at Bangor insisted that all our leaflets had to be printed in Welsh alongside the English (and kindly offered a translation service "at a reasonable cost"); but they were very happy to have their claims paid by cheques written in English...

★★★

Purely from the historical angle, though, the survival here and there of an old language can crop up interestingly. I have a family connection, going back well beyond Victorian days, with a little hamlet in Cornwall called Horningtops. The word 'horning' meant 'iron' in Cornish; and my grandfather's uncle ran the village forge (still there, ruined, at the crossroads). Whoever the travelling census clerk was, visiting with his ink and pen in 1891, he wrote it down as Irontops, no matter what the Ordnance Map said.

Getting back to pronunciation though: sometimes it will stare you in the face but you will be blind to it. I am ashamed to admit (and never have done so until now, and now only because we seem to be getting on so well) that the place in the Firth of Forth, opposite Edinburgh, because it ends in '-land', I saw for years as 'Burntis-land', and so pronounced it on the (thankfully few) occasions it turned up in conversation. They must have thought I was some kind of crank.

I don't want to reveal that ever again…

I drove on…

* * *

And now, almost at once after the gibbet, came that lovely little village Eltisley: sleepy church spire right next to a dream of a half-timbered house, tall and mostly elegant, that must once have been the 'priest-house'; wide village green with a pub at each end of the cricket pitch, sitting enticingly so that after stumps are drawn, the locals can safely crawl to and fro across the grass as necessary through the evening. It is pleasant to envisage rural drunks being harmless and jovial, in contrast to the viciousness we associate with those littering the side-streets of our large towns. Can there be any truth in this? The unwanted image emerged of my brother-in-law, and I quickly headed back to the main road.

I had developed the habit of turning off to Eltisley once or twice a year, just to share for a couple of minutes the gentle peace of villages as they used to be. You can still get this almost anywhere in, say, Herefordshire; but not within fifty miles of London unless you keep very quiet about it.

And you really do have to keep quiet about such concealed oases, when all your impulses – in these days of too much information – are to tell everyone your proud secrets. In the very early Sixties, quite by chance as I was browsing through the Sunday Times small ads., I came across a small cottage for sale on the coast of Southern France – not quite the high-falutin' Riviera but just a few relaxed miles this side of Saint Tropez, which itself was still in the process of being shaken awake by the film industry, and not yet ruined. The vendor was an artist, and Englishman, so the sale could be in sterling and all the crippling foreign exchange restrictions were avoided. I flew out (ah, again the Caravelle!) and did the deal at once: living-room looking across to the Isle of Levant; two small bedrooms, kitchen, shower; large '*cave*' below for table-tennis among the mini-scorpions; some date palms, some cork-oaks; in a tiny *hameau* completely hidden from the coast road and yet on the coastal side of it. Path down to a tiny hidden creek, its pebbles gold and its rocks shining with mica... Why am I telling you all this? I'm damn sure not saying where it is. Oh yes – about keeping quiet...

We did short holiday lets for most of the year when the family weren't using it; and I must tell you, it worked like a dream (well, it *was* a dream) because I got, almost always, the right tenants. My advert., again in the Sunday Times as was only fair, said: "Silent Sunshine, near St. Trop., cottage sleeps 4 by hidden creek; only for quiet people who can keep a secret".

We didn't even have to worry too much about maintenance during the season; Mme Paul in the village had a key and would go in and mop between lettings, but we agreed with each tenant that they must clean up properly, and would only get their deposit back if we had no complaint from their incoming successor. It only went wrong once, when we took a booking from the PA of a famous orchestral conductor. After two days the maestro complained that it wasn't what he had been expecting and he had moved out and wanted his money back...

It transpired that he and a male friend were in the habit of – how can I put it? – (how did *he*, come to think of it!) bumming around along the Riviera, and our local upright French neighbours had taken offence at the arrival of a succession of lithe young boys from the wrong parts of Marseilles. I'll never mention this again, unless somebody will pay me.

⋆⋆⋆

Driving on towards St. Neots, I remembered I had just used the work 'crank' to describe how some folk seem to think of me. I enjoy correcting people, even myself; so I stopped in the lay-by at the market square, turned on the inside light, and reached for the OED which I always carry on the back seat for times like this. I am very happy with this *'Shorter Oxford English Dictionary'* (and have always loved that 'Shorter' which runs to 2515 pages: but nevertheless it would be nice to replace it with the true OED in its twenty volumes: I'll have to buy a bigger car).

My modest distilled version has seven separate listings for 'crank', many of them referring to this or that physical attribute such as 'bent' or 'crooked'; but there are other quite wild references to personal idiosyncrasies: 'a fanciful turn of speech'; 'a rogue who feigns sickness' (interesting as in German '*crank*' means 'ill', does it not?); then we have almost the opposite: 'lively, brisk and merry', however did that happen? And after all that, we get to the verbs: we all know 'to ratchet up', and perhaps that leads on to 'twist and turn about, zigzag', but why 'to capsize' for goodness sake?

At least 'twist and turn' was not inappropriate as I wended my way through that little town and over, at the far end, the bridge across the river. At this stage the Ouse is beginning to grow quite impressively and has that smooth unhurried look I used as a young boy to associate with Kipling's 'grey-green greasy' Limpopo. The Bunny Run will follow the Ouse back, upstream, and across it half-a-dozen-times until – apparently living backwards like Polynesia the Parrot, it has shrunk to a mere stripling, what a poet called 'an old man's jump'.

With Kipling's Limpopo, the greyness, greenness and greasiness have to imagined, because although he sketched the river, he very pleasingly confides in the reader: "I am not allowed to paint these pictures"; it is a nice conceit. He pretends to be terribly upset by the denial and huffs and puffs about it all through the book. A special delight of those *'Just-So Stories'* is how he confides in the reader – when I read them aged about eight, it made me feel quite important.

It is very beneficial for an eight-year old to experience something that makes him or her feel important. It happened to me a couple of times: the first was in Kenya, when my father was a friend of the aged Baden Powell and that old man confided, so I believed, to me in a whisper that his own father had been born in the eighteenth century! The second time? It was on a ship. I'll tell you about it later...

Status, when you are young, can usually be acquired on the sports field, on stage, in a band, or by some other, somewhat abnormal means, perhaps just a single event that will follow you through school. It might even be said that without some such wobbly halo, there is a distinct risk of emerging into the wider world as a nonentity, seeing yourself in that sad light no matter how undeservedly, and remaining so: the storeman or salesman, far beneath the status-blessed Manager, Director, Executive or whatever other title carries its proud capital letter.

***

The road beyond my Limpopo bridge leads quite soon into an old-world village which clings to the narrow space between the Ouse and the present Great North Road, sweeping up dual-carriageway from the Chiltern ridge at Dunstable towards the battlefields of old: Stamford, Newark, East Stoke, Boroughbridge and terrible Towton... I don't know how long ago this great highway superseded the Old North Road that now runs thinly through Ware and Royston (past the old 'royal stone' where they say ancient kings were acclaimed) and which we recently crossed at the gallows; but many splendid coaching inns along the current route will testify to a long history, and one of them, here at Eaton Socon, I was now aiming for: the White Horse.

This was where, as myself a stripling schoolboy, I found

an offbeat way to establish myself, with a positive entity. It was wartime; we were given a surprise long weekend holiday at half-term because some Old Boy had won something; I was well removed from any sports team activities, as usual; and my parents being abroad, I needed to escape from the loving but suffocating grandparents I lived with during the school holidays. So, out of the blue, I booked myself in to the White Horse. Times were not easy just then for country hotels, so I was given the front bow-windowed room above the restaurant, and I believe I was the only guest. Bed-and-breakfast was six-and-sixpence a night. I cycled there on the Friday midday, the dozen-or-so miles, fishing rod tied to my crossbar, and the typewriter and paper dumped in the creaking bike-basket; and settled in for three nights.

What? Yes, my pyjamas and toothbrush and flannel were in my coat pockets, why bring that up? Well, what would you have done, Summer 1944, smart-arse?

Just across the road and down a path, the Ouse swirled past an accessible island, and between the willows was an inviting millpool that was full of the promise of good fat chub... I spent most of the days fishing and caught nothing but weeds; but nearly all night – with nobody's sleep to be disturbed nearby – I typed in my room.

I wrote a play which did catch something: it caught the eye of somebody at the BBC and quite soon they broadcast it: twice, in fact.

At school, to its credit, the pecking order was minimal and unspoken; but I was soon very conscious of my risen position in it, despite my utter lack of sportsfield or gymnasium glamour. This was when I first understood the vital importance of a bit of status, to those who lacked it – and the complete lack of any basic understanding of that problem, by the lucky ones born to be athletic.

This subtle substratum in youthful relationships seldom emerges at primary school level, where opinions and attitudes have not yet crystallised, and in any case one is usually still enjoying the hands-on support and reassurances given by parents. Nevertheless, thinking back to my own earlier years, I came up one day with a story: a bit old-fashioned now, because Africa has changed so much; but they were happy times in my district, it seemed, for most people, whatever their colour, before the boat was rocked. Or certainly it appeared so to the young.

STATUS

From the verandah on a clear day you could see Mount Kilimanjaro – or at least, you could if your Dad lifted you up shoulder-high – and this was a favourite operation in the family because at that distance the mountain looked soft and round and comfortable, like one of Grandma's Christmas puddings back in England.

They always had breakfast on the verandah unless the weather was bad: local fruit-juice followed by Post Toastie cornflakes for him and his mother, which wasn't very adventurous, but his Dad was more experimental in his approach to the tropics, and might have mango or a big grinning slice of paw-paw or other things that looked like melon and tasted like paint.

He was eight. For him, the verandah was the hub of the house, not just their morning meeting-place. It was the back-cloth for his parties and birthday teas, and it was where he laid out his new clockwork train-set with the lead railway-porter and station-master, and the Dinky toys he had brought from home... It was also an exciting place because, though securely part of the house, it opened out on to Africa. The garden, a mere tumble of rough grass so far, sloped down to a rocky stream, then merged into the outer limits of civilized Nairobi: scrubland where you could hear hyenas laughing or jackals snuffling around the rubbish-dumps, as you lay safely under your upstairs mosquito-net at night-time; and where – so the grown-ups would claim over their evening whiskies on your verandah – you might spot the occasional family of lion, cautious and elusive, but still as curious as any other cat when the noises of humans attracted them... (He had heard this when friends came in for a "sundowner", and he – supposed to be on his way to bed – was sitting on the stairs and listening).

He learnt a lot, sitting on the stairs. Grown-up conversation was of limited value but every now and then he might pick up a phrase or an opinion to be retailed at school the next day, dropped into the playtime chatter to gain him a bit of prestige. And this was very necessary, because he was so "new": not just a new boy at school, but new to the Colony. Some of the children in his class came from old-established settler families who had been in Kenya since goodness-knew-when: 1910 or something, before the War. Many others, with parents working for the big Companies, had been born here in the twenties; but his was a Government family sent out only last year in 1935, and in that (certainly at junior schoolboy level) there was a subtle but definite inferiority... He always had to be on the alert for chances to improve his status – sitting on the stairs came to play a vital part in this.

Of course there were others in the same situation, linked in friendship by this mutual feeling of strangeness. Jan, from South Africa, was his closest boy friend. They used to cycle down into the centre of Nairobi together on Saturdays, with their 50 cents pocket-money, and go to the pictures or buy packets of foreign stamps from the little shop at the Newspaper Office opposite the War Memorial. Then they'd ride back and sit in the greenhouse, humming the songs from the Fred Astaire or Dick Powell film they'd seen... "Smoke Gets In Your Eyes"... "I've Been Waiting for an Angel"... and asking each other what it was all about.

Then there was Lottie. At school she shared a desk with him, and that was something special and intimate, leading to all sorts of secrets which must surely be very close to the mysterious sharings his parents did at home? Lottie had come out to Kenya from Germany about the same time as he had come from England. Her father was some sort of official with a very funny accent, but *her* English was perfect by now, and together they tried to pick up Swahili. It was fun, learning the words alongside your parents, being quicker at it than them, being able to call the gardener the "*shamba-boy*" and knowing what was wanted from the tool-shed when he sent you to find a "*panga*" for cutting back the undergrowth. The house-boys used to call him the "*Bwana Kidogo*" which was "The little Boss" and out-and-out flattery: behind your back they had vivid and sometimes unrepeatable nicknames for you all, and usually your Dad knew about it and it was taken in good part all round... In those days there seemed a good working relationship.

He used to meet Lottie before school every morning, at the bus-stop. Now he was eight, he could go that far by himself, down the rough-made road and over the railway-crossing... Big steam-rollers were at work on the road, crushing down the sprawling heaps of "*murrum*", a red bubbly stone for road-making, not at all smooth and boring like the tarmac of London streets, but strange rounded knobs of loose crunchy stuff that had come out of volcanoes – that was another fact he had learnt while sitting on the stairs, and at school some of the big boys had spoken to him kindly after he had passed this knowledge on, one break-time. But they all used to walk through the murrum carelessly, scuffing their feet, and of course his mother wouldn't let him do that with his new shoes, so the friendliness from the seniors had been a bit tenuous and died out by the next day.

Sometimes he got to the bus-stop first, sometimes Lottie. The level-crossing was an exciting place because you could see the massive railway-engines with their hooters and their cow-catchers like a row of shining oily teeth, as they heaved their trucks and their sleeping-cars up from Mombasa through the capital, bound for the hinterland and Lake Victoria... Vast clouds of grey smoke puffed out from the wood logs that fuelled them. Once at night-time, coming back from school extra late for some reason, they had sat in the bus while the up-train struggled past in the darkness, wheezing like an old man, and the sky was a whirlwind of burning red sparks, weaving and shining like a swarm of fire-flies, and Lottie had grabbed his hand in wonder as they watched it go by.

As he stood waiting at the bus-stop, the long straggle of native women would come past, bearing on their heads an endless assortment of goods to market. From hooks in their ears hung long copper bangles which swung and glinted as they walked, and many were going to get into trouble in the town when the askaris saw them, because nearly always those copper wires had been stolen from the new telegraph-poles up-country – fashion having always had the edge on technology. But whatever the police might say or do, the women were always cheerful and glided jauntily along, chewing at long sticks of sugar-cane which they would spit out on to the side of the road when the juice had all gone, so that you could always identify a main road into Nairobi from the villages by the endless trail along its verges of dry white chewed sugar-cane.

By now, he could recognise some of the women, with their funny scarred lines and patterns on their cheeks, tribal marks which were just as natural as your mother's lipstick once you got used to the idea. And one girl in particular, in an orange frock, with a lean swinging figure and a nice face, had once smiled at him and offered him a stick of sugar-cane but he had been too shy to take it; so an older boy from a settler family got it instead... She had looked back then and smiled at him again, and he hadn't known whether to feel big or small.

It was only a short journey on the bus; then he and Lottie would take the path across a field of mealies to reach the school gates. Back in England he had never heard of mealies, and it was the shock of his life when an American boy told him it was just maize, what you make corn-flakes with, and another friend had said: "No, that is Indian Corn", but whatever it was, the very hugeness of it in the field, growing way above their heads, was always a bit awe-inspiring when he remembered the gentle Sussex cornfields he could see across at shoulder-height.

In the centre of the mealie-field stood a shabby bungalow-style farm-house, where a man lived who was Lottie's uncle. He had been there since the early days of German East Africa, and he was thin and weather-beaten and his khaki shirt and shorts hung on him much as the dry leaves hung down from the mealies... They used to call Hello to him on their way to school, hurrying past in fear of a rap across the knuckles from Miss Logan's ruler if they were late for assembly... But on the way home they would dawdle, and play "house" in the lean-to shed at the back of the old man's bungalow. It was there that he told her, one day soon after a Fred Astaire film, that he was going to marry her when they grew up; and then she had happened to find a brass curtain-ring lying on a shelf, and gave it to him to put on her finger; and after he had done that, they had agreed to keep the whole thing a secret, and together they hid the ring in a knot-hole in the wall before going for their bus. And there it stayed: always, whenever they looked to make sure.

As time went on and their friendship deepened, he used to share with Lottie any special news he had learnt on the stairs the previous evening: it was a way of showing his affection; and indeed, apart from Dinky toys which were too masculine, and caterpillars which had lost their appeal for her after one got squashed underfoot in the shed, information was the most valuable thing he had to offer. It sometimes paid off, when they bore extra-special tidings to the playground: like a very early occasion when the old King had died and Edward VIII came to the Throne, and sitting on the terrace in the January sunshine they thoughtfully told their assembled listeners how at least one good thing would come of it – certainly the Silver Jubilee stamps would go up in value...

But the new year developed badly. With the passing months, the grown-ups were changing. Gradually they seemed to lose the happiness of their chatter in the evenings on his verandah: more and more, the talk would be serious, voices lowered when they sensed him on the stairs. Once, when he was found there by Kitau the house-boy who was usually an ally, his mother was alerted and he was bundled off upstairs in almost public disgrace... This was bewildering. He could read the newspaper headlines of course, as they waved at him in the mornings across the table and the paw-paw; and he came to recognise words and comments from overheard conversations, like Rhineland, Austria, Italy, Hitler, Abyssinia... It meant very little.

But then, at school the other boys began to notice his lack of new information: he was no longer an authority on items of interest. One of the others even had to tell *him* that there had been an invasion, some time ago, of Abyssinia which was the bordering country to the North. He was losing his prestige... And if that went, since he had no particular compensating prowess at cricket, football, on the rifle-range, even in the classroom, there was a danger of his losing the devotion of Lottie. True, she had shown no sign of disaffection, but she was certainly seeming a little unhappy nowadays, and at their morning meetings one sometimes saw signs of recent tears, hints of trouble at home. He knew that a master-stroke was needed, and without delay.

That weekend, for the first time ever, he politely declined to go with his parents on their drive out to watch game on the plains. The heavy old box-body car with its big spotlight above the driver's window, would park at a likely spot near the water-holes. Zebra, buck, giraffe, and wildebeest were commonplace of course, and over the other side of town where it was even dustier, ostriches. Also, when your luck was in, you might see lion and leopards; and failing all that, there was always the four-engined biplane that arrived every Sunday with the week's mail from Croydon... A social event: meet the plane, meet your friends.

But this time, No Thank-you, he would like to stay in the house and do his stamps; and his parents smiled over the top of his head and thought how he was growing up and developing that charming yet hateful blasé independence we all get when we are coming up to nine. With Kitau and the shamba-boy near at hand, he would be quite all right; so off they drove for the evening, and he waved to them past the orange trees and down the red lumpy road.

Then, he went and gathered up all the newspapers he could find; he turned on the wireless to hear the News: ("Seven L.O. Nairobi Kenya calling"), and he studied Current Affairs as if a scholarship depended upon it. True, he read chiefly the headlines; but there were maps, and commentaries which he could understand, and there were captions to photographs of fierce men marching about in a goose-step and feeble-looking ones lying down… With his Bartholomew School Atlas open on the carpet beside him, it all began to make some sense. By the time his parents returned for supper, full of the thrill of seeing a leopard in a tree with its kill, he had his own Big Story quite clear in his head, he had tidied up the papers, and he was back on the carpet with his stamp collection.

On Monday morning at the bus-stop he told Lottie all about the world situation. She listened quietly. He was very wrapped-up in the urgency of it all, and if she sat there twisting her pigtail and biting her lip, he didn't notice. In "break", he caught the attention of the bigger boys by commenting upon the stupidity, of any country that had to print postage-stamps for 10,000,000 marks or ten million anything; he said that if they had done that after the Great War, who knew what other dangerous things they might get up to… This wasn't challenged, so he went on to say how everybody was worried about another War coming: it was all the fault of the Germans again, they were marching into other people's countries, and killing everybody, and this was the Biggest News Ever but the grown-ups wouldn't tell the children about it, yet it was happening and soon there would be tanks again and poison gas and aeroplane dog-fights like it said in those old War Illustrated books in the library, and it was the Germans doing it all.

Most of the lunch-break he answered questions, even from some of the biggest boys. One of them walked back to the bus with him after school, and another invited him to play on Saturday. Lottie wasn't there because she had been sick and gone home early... but girls are a bit stupid anyway, said the older boy.

She wasn't at the bus next morning either, and her mother had sent a message to say she was ill. But when he passed through their mealie-field that afternoon, he slipped through the fence into their special shed, and she was there: sitting in the dark, on her own, crying a little, with the brass curtain-ring on her finger...

No, she wasn't coming back to the school, she told him. She had been ordered not to talk to him again, and her uncle in the khaki shorts was terribly angry, and anyway they were going back home to Europe soon, and she thought it best if he just please took the curtain-ring and kept it to remember her by.

So he took the grubby brass ring silently from her finger. Somehow he knew that something terrible was happening, that he had helped to bring it about... but he couldn't quite work out what it was... It was like the part of a film, near the end, where everything goes wrong momentarily... but in the film it all came out right in the end.

Therefore, he thought, there can't be anything to worry about in the long run. And they agreed about that, and they promised to write and to send each other all the new stamp issues that came out – even if they are a thousand million marks, he joked – and then he got up and trudged off alone through the mealie-field without looking back, like he'd seen at the pictures with Jan.

It was late afternoon now, as he walked towards the bus-stop, and the usual native women were trailing back from market with their baskets empty on their heads. He felt an unusual kind of loneliness as he clutched his brass ring, a sense that somehow things were changing... He knew that the day was coming, when he could no longer be a listener sitting on the stairs, but would have to join the grown-ups who occupied his verandah in the evenings, would have to share not only their sun-downers but all the worries of their world, too...

The slender young woman in the orange frock had sold her load of bananas, and came smiling past. As she reached him, they looked at each other and she stopped for a moment, seeing distress in his eyes.

"*Jambo*", she said – Hello – and held out a piece of sugar-cane.

This time he took it without hesitation. Then he noticed that she had lost the copper bangles from her ears.

"*Jambo*", he replied; and he opened his hand to her with the curtain-ring in it.

With a big grin she took it from him. "*Santa sana*",

she said – Thank you – and putting it to her ear she swung away towards her village.

He strolled on, up the dusty road with his satchel, spitting out sugar-cane and scuffing his new shoes in the murrum like anything.

IV

The road to Clear Blue Sky

I stopped off just now at the White Horse for three good reasons (I'd like to have made it seven but didn't have the time): first, pure nostalgia – the older we get, the more vivid the past seems to become, perhaps in compensation for our encroaching loss of memory, so that ultimately it is often the only comfortable place to live; second, I needed a really stiff drink after my horrid family experience that day; and thirdly, I had decided to phone home…

Ah, but wait a moment: fourthly, I needed the loo; fifthly, for old time's sake I wanted to re-visit upstairs the hotel part of the place; how can I make this up to my lucky seven? Well, six, I thought I might chat up the barmaid… And – yes! – I ought to check my tyres. Now I feel better…

After a couple of Scotches I told the girl I wanted to ring home, and she directed me to a payphone in the far dark corner. I held on for a few minutes as it rang, but was not really very surprised when there was no answer.

"Thanks, no reply, bye-bye Sylvia," I called.

"Do you have far to go?" I told her: Oxford.

"Mind how you go – what's it, about sixty miles?"

"Sixty-three," I corrected her, as one does. She was a nice girl and I made a mental note... Now that I was free...

I crunched across their newly-relaid gravel and shortly turned off westwards towards Bedford. This was a section of the Bunny Run I knew particularly well, gentle hills with the river still close to me on the left. One stretch of it always brought back to mind a very wintry day when, right ahead of me, a motor-bike skidded on black ice and ended up in the hedge. After I helped him out he told me this story:

A man and his pillion-passenger set out on a freezing day and as driver, he decided to counter the cold by wearing his overcoat back to front; he also pulled his cap down with its peak at the back so that it wouldn't blow off... They crashed. When the passenger came round, he walked across to the small crowd that had gathered around his friend. "Is he all right?" he asked. The rescuer-in-charge said: "He's much quieter now but we had a hell of a job getting his head round the right way."

This in turn always reminds me of that other story about people who mean well:

A worker from Poland who spoke no English, fell ill and was visited in hospital by his mate who spoke no Polish. Soon after arriving, he was alarmed to see the Pole's condition deteriorating: the poor man was clearly at death's door. The visitor felt that, with nobody else around, the least he could do was to record his last words, so he wrote them down as they were repeatedly gasped: "Przybozkyzxy" or words to that effect. At the funeral he asked one of his countrymen what it meant. "You are sitting on my breathing tube."

Another mile, and there is a spot where once upon a time the air would have been thick with last words: this was the Viking attack on Bedford, which was then a border town. The invading Danes sailed right up the Ouse. They dug themselves a very efficient dock a few miles downstream, leaving us some interesting earthworks upon which the avid Victorian railway magnates planted a station, believe it or not! Equally dismissive of most events prior to 1066, the Ordnance Survey mappers can't be bothered with the Battle of Bedford (no crossed swords) and even describe as a mere 'earthwork' the silent and evocative mound that stands beside the road overlooking the flat riverside meadows, and containing, so I believe, the bodies of the dead invaders. The castle at Bedford itself, perched upon the Ouse, must have been a powerful one and well defended: evidently it stopped the "great hairy men as huge as sin, with horned heads" who, we are vividly told by Chesterton, "came wading in, from the sunrise and the sea." What a man that was, as fiery as those he wrote about.

After doffing my cap at that old burial-mound, a short way further on there is a turning to my left, which runs straight as a Saxon arrow to one of my favourite Ouse bridges, Great Barford with the water gliding silently through waving water-weeds that seem to stroke it past; one can imagine those longboats equally quietly slipping up in the other direction, with muffled oars, so long ago.

From the final hill, away in the distance, miles beyond

the river, there is a quick glimpse of the gigantic airship sheds of Cardington, standing as a gloomy grey memorial to what, at the time, seemed a good idea: those ill-fated dirigibles R100 and R101. We were never as clever as the Germans in constructing those floating time-bombs, and after R101 crashed and then even the Graf Zeppelin folded up so spectacularly, everybody involved in the trade went rather quiet... But whyever did it take so long to recognise their vulnerability? Surely to goodness, once that chap in his little plane had won his VC for shooting down a Zeppelin over London in 1916, people should have seen the limitations?

And then another minor thought: what an ugly word 'dirigible' is. Nobody ever seems to have bothered to find a more pleasing one. You can't call them all Zeppelins any more than you can call everything you push around the carpet a Hoover. 'Airship' was a good start, except that nowadays one expects a 'ship' to have thousands of passengers and nearly that many fawning crew. As for that 'dirigible' word itself: all it means is "capable of being directed" – how boring – and how vague! It's a great pity, perhaps that 'Silver Cloud' has been bagged by Rolls-Royce.

I'm sure that in many people's minds, 'dirigible' links with 'risible'; what a pity. At any rate, when the 1939-45 war came along, Cardington's sheds became the headquarters for a different kind of balloon that was not risible at all: the more modest barrage-balloons we all grew accustomed to as a sort of umbrella against air attack. I could see the sheds from my classroom window, and balloons being experimented with in various ways, upside-down, on end, varying shapes... There were usually about half-a-dozen of them, silver against the breakfast sky; I would count them every morning and if there were seven it was going to be a good day.

Needless to say, there were plenty of other things up in the sky at that time; and as I look back I am amazed to remember how laidback we were, as teenagers. I was sauntering up to school one morning when, quite casually out of low cloud and without any air-raid warning, a Dornier chugged across the town over my head and dropped a handful of bombs on the railway station... Then he was away again, perfectly calmly into the cloud, back to his hausfrau and his sauerkraut... I don't even remember anyone talking about it.

There was something else that added to my curiously happy memories of those days, though of such awful anguish to the grown-ups: after Easter or thereabouts, the clocks were to be put back – no forward – two hours rather than just one, to give us Double Summer Time. This was supposed to be enormously helpful to the War Effort because the factory workers – erm, wait a minute – would either leap out of bed in glorious sunshine and grope their way home for supper, or... No, hang on: go to work in the dark, but enjoy a long sunlit evening while the bombers amassed overhead.

It must have been the latter, because in my dormitory we used to lie dreamily in our fully daylit beds listening to the French romantics on Radio Luxembourg, whom I have already talked about...

Luxembourg filled a gap, a teenage void, that would later and belatedly be occupied by the offshore Channel pirates and at last by a reluctant BBC's Radio One. It was a splendid operation, always eccentric and wide open to imitation, with its sudden advertisement ejaculations. By far the best skit on Luxembourg was a 78 recording made by a brilliant man of the Thirties whom nobody seems to remember: Peter Taunton. His *'Radio Boloni'* is a joy. There is a spoof thriller where the hero gets killed by mistake in the first episode; there is the advertisement which offers a 'completely free' gift to anyone enclosing "a tee-shilling poose, er, a pee-shilling toose – er – one-and-elevenpence". Best of all, a recipe starts: "Take a pint of water and beat it to a stiff cream..."

We listened to jazz, too. This was when the rhythm of it was a basic primeval appeal, and before all those clever-clever modernists "improved" it beyond the understanding of the man in the street, as they have with nearly all the Arts. It must have been great to be – say – the trombonist at a real old New Orleans wake. It must be good to play the trombone...

Or any such instrument, but only here and there. I mean by this that there are so many brief passages of my favourite pieces of music where I long to join in – but always in a different section of the orchestra. Not the piano: when I was a child at that Kenya primary school you've just read about (or skipped), the music teacher was a vicious old Irish woman who, if I played a wrong note on her diseased piano, would crack me across the knuckles with the edge of a ruler. Hard. That rather pointed me towards the triangle-and-tambourine section, the kitchen crowd.

But how wonderful to be behind the tympani, or in the middle of a herd of them, for the final bars of Elgar's 'Cockaigne'. Or have the lead clarinet part (I think it must be, but I'll check and let you know) in the 'Barber of Seville' overture for that little twiddly bit right at the end of the main melody, and I'm sure Rossini meant that flourish to be louder: many conductors seem dedicated to drowning it out, but it ties up the whole phrase so neatly. And I'll tell you something else about destructive conductors: it's disgraceful how often they destroy the wonder of the 'Rosenkavalier' waltz sequence by suffocating the trumpet at that triumphant point of four rising notes... Are they daft, or just being superior and – literally – avoiding 'playing to the gallery'? Handel knew better: look at the 'Halleluia chorus' trumpet.

These snippets of sound come across better actually in the room, as I was so lucky to be when the BBC Orchestras broadcast from my School almost every day – and let us go in to listen – through a couple of the war years. I was too young to worry about such finer points, and I'm not much advanced even now; but I do remember very vividly, in 'Scheherezade' at the Albert Hall many years ago, how that sensational single stroke on the tam-tam reverberated around the building like the start of an earthquake – yet when you listen to that piece on the radio, it is almost completely lost...

It was strange, I suppose, how ordinary life went on during the war, for those not actually hit by it. Even the grown-ups, most of them for most of the time, pressed on: "Business as usual" signs hanging lopsided from the shattered window-frames of your local grocer. "Sausages tomorrow" was stuck on the door of our butcher for a full five years until that tomorrow eventually came. And we teenagers in the blitzed South-East, found a new and exciting collecting hobby: jagged pieces of shrapnel with edges as prickly as a steel hedgehog; spent cartridges, sometimes even unexploded cannon-shells (my pal Hilditch was filing away at one at the back of the classroom and it blew his finger off – great! A taste of real war!). We didn't read the papers, or if we did, we skipped the serious bits; we half expected to be invaded, but we laughed it off. Don't people still do that, as a gut reaction to underlying fear?

Later in the war, I cycled home at the end of one Term, taking four days over it by avoiding the mayhem of London; and this is more or less what happened.

CLEAR BLUE SKY

There were vapour trails in the summer sky above him; and as he free-wheeled downhill between high ancient hedgerows, he would sometimes have to shut his eyes before a cloud of dizzy mayflies which danced and capered away their precious hours in the sunshine. At last, the high wavy edge of the Chilterns appeared on the skyline; and somewhere along there beyond Wantage, the old track led to White Horse Hill…

"Before the Gods who made the gods had seen their

sunrise pass, the White Horse of the White Horse Hill was cut out of the grass..." That was how G.K. Chesterton had put it, and two years ago, back in the Fourth Form, the poem had captured his imagination. He carried the book with him now on this voyage of juvenile discovery, in his bike-basket along with the Ordnance Survey maps and the Cadet Force haversack with his pyjamas and toothbrush. It had taken him two days so far, the start of the Summer Holidays, to cycle here from School on his roundabout journey home to Surrey.

His grandparents, of course, were against it (he lived with them because of the War, Mum and Dad being the other side of the world on Government work ever since 1939). Very long faces had been pulled... "Don't you *like* coming home to us in the holidays?" was suggested, if never actually said. But he was nearly seventeen now; well, over sixteen anyway; and at eighteen boys were in the Forces...

Look, he had said to them, it's 1945 and the War's practically over. If it hadn't ended, I would have been away fighting within a year or so, and we've been saved that worry... Secondly, because of the War I've had no chance to travel about and see things, so it's high time I did. And thirdly, I get a bit bored sitting about all the hols. with you, doing the shopping, watching Grandad do the garden, and going to Church on Sunday. So if you can just wire me ten pounds I'll be entirely self-supporting on this adventure; and I'll be home for supper on Friday.

As soon as the boredom of Speech Day was over,

off he had set. Across Bedfordshire and Buckingham the first day, with supper-bed-and-breakfast that first night in a tiny thatched cottage north of Aylesbury, for six-and-sixpence; he had to go easy because by some mistake or other Grandad had only sent eight pounds... But the second night he gave in to the temptation of the most gorgeous old private hotel near the Thames in Oxfordshire where bed-and-breakfast, even without the evening meal, was sixteen shillings: he had woken in the morning, amid the luxury of a huge feather-bed and mellow oak furniture, in a sweat of nerves in case his money wouldn't see him safely back to Surrey by the weekend... But good manners overcame misgivings and he still remembered to leave a shilling for the chambermaid before pedalling off into Berkshire.

* * *

It was a splendid day, reminding him of that wonderful Summer of 1940 with all its excitements and the weaving pattern of planes duelling in the sky. A few miles short of Wantage he took another step towards manhood and stopped at a pub for the first time in his life... The bar was empty, all copper and flagstones, and the landlord served him his half-pint of mild without questioning his age. Yes, he said, you'll come straight to the White Horse if you follow the road out of Wantage towards Swindon; but there won't be anyplace to stay, so Wantage is the best bet... Thank you, Sir, and good day.

And in Wantage, the hotel in the Square, big and pricey and full-up, directed him to a possible haven:

"Turn left at the cross-roads, love, and try No. 23 – they often do b-and-b to help us out"...

Number 23 was one of the shabbiest old Georgian houses he had ever seen: the sort of genteel decadent home you can find two of, in so many half-forgotten villages: one used to be the vicar, and the other the Doctor, but they've both moved on, amalgamated with other villages, and the houses quietly slid into decline... But here there was a whole row of them, and they sat behind their overgrown hawthorn hedge with its intrusive eldertrees, dreaming of the past and shouting silently for love and a coat of paint.

A cheerful little woman opened the door to his knock, and showed him up to a room badly overcrowded by stacks of furniture. He agreed b-and-b for ten shillings with a light supper thrown in; and then, as it was past mid-day, he headed for the White Horse Hill, to be back by six.

Sausage and beans at the cafe in Wantage was one-and-ninepence, washed down with Tizer; then the road ran along the skirt of the hillside, curving in and out of its downward folds, through clusters of giant beech-trees. At last he struggled up the great climb that led to the White Horse, and explored the sleeping green embankments of Iron Age men which the maps call Uffington Castle; and at last, with Chesterton's book in his hand, he dozed on the turf at the crest of the hill – the weird Horse at his feet and a dozen skylarks in the blueness above him.

As he stretched back and looked at the sky, his sun-hazy mind drifted with the clouds, back across History;

he heard the blast of King Alfred's rallying-call which had summoned the faithful to battle fifteen hundred years ago… And up in that same blue sky, in and out of those fleecy clouds just five years ago, he remembered the excitements and the dog-fights: "Red Leader calling… Bandits ten thousand…" Then the rattle of guns and the parachutes… And the souvenirs to hunt for afterwards on Epsom Downs or Walton Heath… What a time to be alive, he thought; and through the afternoon he lay there dreaming.

⋆⋆⋆

A funny old place, Wantage, he decided as he cycled back at six o'clock. Ploughing their fields, milking their cows, no sign of a War, no bomb damage, nothing.

"I bet you weren't short of butter and eggs down here," he said at supper-time, and they smiled and agreed with him. There was the little woman who had met him before; and her daughter, about a year younger than himself, dark hair that hung down nicely, and unusual violet eyes. She had been in the front drive as he skimmed in for supper, alongside a smallish horse.

"This is Angela," the mother had told him. "She's learning to ride".

He had said, rather cleverly: "I thought everybody named Angela could ride straight from the cradle".

"I'm a late developer," the girl retorted over her shoulder as she led the animal away.

Supper was largely a matter of cheese and pickles, but after his achievements of the day, very welcome nevertheless. They talked a lot: they were interested to hear all about his journey, his School, his plans for the future.

Angela, it appeared, was doing English Literature for her Higher Certificate – as he was. This, too, gave them something to talk about; and as the evening went on he found himself warming to her, giving her a few helpful hints about Keats and Robert Browning and generally – he felt – acting as a decent Sixth-Former should to a younger girl: he didn't know much about girls, mind you, but this one was decidedly all right.

The two of them got his map out after the table had been cleared, and planned an interesting route for him to follow tomorrow, as he unwound his way Eastwards towards Surrey. Angela was quite keen on History and castles and battlefields, as he was; and she went and found two funny little brass measuring-wheels which you pushed across the map, following the route, so you could measure the distances. She used one, and he the other, and it got quite good fun trundling them across the page to work out the mileage. They started betting on whose guess was closest, with a box of matches each and a stake of five matches a time, and a good deal of laughter.

When he had won nearly all the matches, he said to her boldly: "Really, you know, you shouldn't be buried away down here – with nothing to do all the time. I suppose it's useful learning to ride a horse and all that, but honestly – does anything ever happen?"

She ran a hand through that long hair but didn't answer at first. Then, defensively: "Why should people *want* things to *happen* all the time?"

"In London," he said, "there's so much going on. Even when the War and the raids were on, that's were it all actually happened – all the excitement, seeing it all. I wouldn't have missed it for the world".

"Missed it?" Her mother looked up from her sewing across the room, over her glasses. "Don't you think it was a good thing to have missed it?"

"Heavens," he said, "it was thrilling. I used to stand out in the garden day after day, in the Summer of 1940, and see that clear blue sky dotted all over with little shining specks, the Germans coming in in waves; and then you'd see the tiny V-formations of Spitfires and Hurricanes swooping in on them, and high up all the machine-gun bursts and then the start of vertical smoke-trails and there would be a plane spinning down like a falling leaf, sometimes terribly slowly, sometimes with a long line of black smoke behind it, and then the parachutes would open – or anyway, usually they would – and on the News that night Joseph MacLeod or Bruce Belfrage or some other newsreader would say how many we'd shot down and how many we'd lost…"

They had put down their sewing and the road-map, and were listening, absorbed. "It sounds fantastic," said Angela. "You really saw all that?"

"Then later on," he continued, "when the night-time Blitz started, that was like a never-ending Guy Fawkes Night. I'd look out of my bedroom window, down there in Surrey, and see the deep red glow all along the skyline over Central London, with a sudden white flare-up when another stick of bombs went down, and a heavy distant wumping sound; and all the time, up above, you'd have the flashes of ack-ack fire like rockets, and the searchlights would be flailing about and swinging across the sky and if you were really lucky you'd see a Jerry caught in the beam of the light… It was like a sort of fairyland."

He stopped for breath. The woman looked at him, surprised. "Fairyland?"

Angela glanced at her mother. "He means History," she said, "That's all. Fairyland and History are part of the same thing, Mummy – look at King Alfred".

"Arthur." He corrected her. "Arthur was the mythical one".

She swung round on him very suddenly, and her violet eyes were flashing. "You're quite a nice boy," she said, "but you're a knowall. I said *Alfred*."

"Well anyway," her mother put in quickly, "History is made in Wantage as well as in London, no doubt; but bed-time is world-wide, and this is it."

On the stairs she turned to him. "It must have been rather magical, all those panoramic lights and bangs and flashes: an experience for you to remember, I can understand that, and it would be wrong to forget it; but you ought to be thankful for peaceful nights now."

He squeezed into his bedroom with its overwhelming clutter of Victoriana, and soon he was drifting among the green hills and the blue skies that housed the Gods who made the Gods, till morning.

⋆ ⋆ ⋆

Due to leave after breakfast, he was craning over the road-map next to Angela at the table when something new happened to him: a tiny animal shock as she leaned close, looking for Reigate, and her delicious hair brushed against his face.

She, of course, noticed nothing: too young. Nevertheless he would like to see her again… Surreptitiously he slipped into his pocket one of the little brass wheels; when he got home he could post it back with a note saying how it must have happened by accident, and could they meet if ever she ventured up to the Big City… This, with its possible spin-off and developments, struck him as an exceptionally bold idea – how debonair she would think him!

He went to pack; and later he was stuffing everything into his bike-basket as she happened along, leading her horse. "I'm glad you came," she said, "perhaps you'll be back one day?"

He doubted it; and asked if she was ever up in Town; but she shook her head. "Mummy doesn't like London now," she said. Clumsily, she got up on the horse, and set off at a snail's pace down the lane.

He called after her, pointing in the other direction. "Ghent's that way," and she laughed beautifully.

She was almost out of earshot when she drew up and turned in the saddle. "By the way, I've lost one of those brass wheel things – let me know if you can find one in London." And she lurched off gingerly round the bend.

Her mother said Goodbye to him. "What have you learnt," she asked, "from the White Horse?" He was uncertain and waited for her to go on…

"You can't judge things from the distance," she said, and she was looking at him very seriously, like a schoolteacher almost. "It looks beautiful from faraway, but when you're in the middle of it you can't see it and you just get your feet dirty... She looked down at him, poised on his bike. "Look at you: your head's in the blue sky, and your feet are all covered in dirty chalk..." She smiled, and ruffled his hair; and he was off.

⋆ ⋆ ⋆

After a few miles, and at the same pub as before, he went in from the fierce sunshine for a quick one: this time he felt a good deal more mature than the callow youth of yesterday, and called for a pint of bitter, which gave him time to chat to the landlord.

Yes, he had found bed-and-breakfast in Wantage: he described the place. Nice people, but perhaps a bit unworldly...?

Yes, said the Landlord, nice people. Newcomers.

Newcomers?

From London, bombed out in the Blitz... Beautiful house in North London: they'd rescued some furniture from the rubble, that's all... They were saved, sheltering under the stairs, but the young son had been killed – he was looking out of the window at the flashes and searchlights... Very sad really, because the elder boy had been shot down in the Battle of Britain. But there you are, said the Landlord, it happened all the time. Life has to go on somehow, somewhere – so why not Wantage?

⋆ ⋆ ⋆

In the middle of it, he remembered, you just get your feet dirty... Oh, God! Oh, Christ! What have I said?

He left his frightfully grown-up drink; and he sped to the nearest railway-station, and went swiftly, silently home.

Late that evening, he sat upstairs wretchedly in his room, and looked at the bloody-stupid swollen-headed self-centred face in the mirror... What could they have been thinking of him, spouting his smart-alick opinions and his absurd precocious chatter?

And Angela: she would never want to see him again – how she must have been hating him, despite all the politeness. Clearly he must forget all about her, just post back the brass measuring-wheel with a brief note – or better, no comment at all except the one word "Sorry" – that would say it all.

Sadly he reached into his pocket and felt around; and then, catching his breath, he brought out his hand and in it, shining at him, were *two* little brass wheels.

V

The road to Mr Hertzog

Well, OK, in real life there was only the one wheel in my pocket; but that was enough for me to keep in touch, and I'll never forget those violet eyes... Moving on from them was sad, but inevitable. The Army carries its own in-house attractions, and young subalterns soon succumb to the lubrications of the gin-and-orange circuit.

But now, here I was again moving on. I decided to telephone my brother-in-law, assuming that at this hour of the evening (it was only just dark) he wasn't yet drunk, nor robbing people in the back-streets. I drove around Bedford looking for a phone-box.

The Embankment at Bedford is the making of the town, and the finest use of its river, so far as I know, of any stretch of the Ouse. Just past the site of the castle, that target for the marauders, we come to the Town Bridge, where in mid-stream since the middle ages, had stood the town gaol; where John Bunyan sat sharpening his quill and dreaming his dream. A very sensible place to site one's prison – they did the same downriver at St. Ives, or is that one a chapel? Maybe both, in its time.

I have seven – yes, I know – favourite Ouse bridges. I'll tell you about them because it won't take long and you know about some already, like St Ives, St Neots, Great Barford and now Bedford. I will be crossing the other three in the next half-hour's drive so I'd better be getting along.

Here, by a stone horse-trough, was the spot where I was once knocked off my feet by a passing bicycle and – shamefully – wet myself, right down into my Wellington boots (it was winter and icy) – I'll never forget that squelching back to the boarding house... Over there was the home of a friend whose family had unearthed from the riverbank a rotten wooden chest full of Roman coins: I went and saw it yearningly but they didn't offer me one...

And then, heading out of town, the prison; a big, solemn high-walled place designed to accommodate the miscreants of today. Many times longer than the entire Town Bridge, let alone the tiny chamber that had apparently been sufficient for malefactors in Good King Charles' gilded days – or was that because they would simply have been strung up to save the cost of their board and lodging?

I found a phone-box, while wondering how much the taxpayer had been stung, over the years, by my wife's brother. Twice inside for theft, once for GBH. Cautioned three times for various outbursts of temper with damaging results... Carrying a weapon with intent...

And now he had been showing signs of menace towards his own sister, just because she had inherited. And yet...

She had herself become so difficult, so lacking in any real understanding, that despite myself I was beginning to detect a rare hint of reluctant sympathy for the man. After all, he had taken his share of care of the old lady their mother, when he wasn't locked up somewhere; so even I could appreciate that he deserved some share in the inheritance, and had made it clear. My wife was a cruel and selfish woman. How should I phrase this phone-call?

I was on the western side of the town. And because, right down Western Europe's seaboard, and throughout history, that was the superior region to live (avoiding the smells and toxins blown through the streets by the prevailing wind) and still retained that aura of up-marketness, the telephone had not been vandalised in its box.

"Hello," I said, "I've been ringing home and getting no reply. Do you think you could –."

"I hate the woman."

"Yes, OK, I know all about that; but I have to ask you, because at the end of the day, this is 'family'; I'm just asking you to go round and see if everything's all right."

"Why would it not be?"

"Well," I replied a little awkwardly, "the truth it, we had a bit of a row – ."

"That's not difficult."

"Yes, but it was a slight misunderstanding, and I think she isn't speaking to me. So be a good chap and go round to make sure she's OK. I'm over in Oxford, you see, as usual this time of the week, and there's nobody else I could ask at this hour of the night." And I added as an afterthought "She was talking about arranging to give you a good share of your Mum's money – I think it would be sensible."

"Yeah, OK," he said. "I'll go over there. Can I ring you back?"

I told him I would ring my home number in an hour and could he please stay at my place until then.

"I haven't got a key," he pointed out, just in case she wouldn't answer the door: it had happened before.

"I've thought of that. The bay window on the left, beside the front door, is always on the latch."

"OK then, call me in an hour or so – I'll hang about and perhaps talk some sense into her."

Rather doubting that, I hung up.

* * *

Very soon I came to another of my favourite Ouse bridges, at Bromham where it must date back hundreds of years, with its little alcoves into which one can imagine children and travelling tinkers diving to avoid a galloping stage-coach… Or a bumptious 1930s charabanc… Or indeed my Sunbeam-Talbot, I confess, because there was no speed limit.

Many of the village churches around Bedford have a square tower topped by a mini-spire, usually central. This is a very local feature, as a lively teacher once explained to us; and I remember shortly afterwards browsing through a copy of Punch and seeing a cartoon which included just such a church; and doing a bit of research, which resulted in identifying the artist as being indeed a local resident. I was proud of this and asked a lot of my friends to guess which region of the country that was portrayed in the drawing. It was enjoyable to correct them all.

But I was moving out of that area swiftly. I reflected that years before, in the Army, I had once given a ten-minute lecture as part of my OCTU course; we were allowed to choose our own subject and mine was: "Knowing where you are". It set out to prove, or at least to claim, that if you were dropped by parachute anywhere in the English countryside, you should be able to know where you had landed, to within thirty miles, just by looking around you. Sometimes it would be easiest to judge by the crops: the flat black fields of celery would suggest East Anglia, or there is the famous rhubarb triangle east of Sheffield, or more specialist still, Betjeman's 'licorice fields at Pontefract', although I had already given my talk by the time he published his poem. Then, the construction of the older buildings: the locally handmade bricks of the Weald, the heavy black-and-white of the Welsh border, or – East Anglia again – the external plasterwork on timbered buildings or brick-built farms with an erratic edge influenced by the Dutch just across the water. Different ways of plaiting their hedges, of weaving and decorating their thatch, or putting together their stone walls. The mini-spire of Bedford churches I have already mentioned, if you were paying attention… Then the soil itself: I am hopelessly ignorant of the North (why don't the Pennines go sideways?) – but down South, England tilts up from Cornwall, so far as I can see, and after its solid old granite we get the red earth of Devon, sometimes almost impossibly red after a downpour; as we edge through the strata eastwards, we end up with the chalk, which is the youngest deposit and is guaranteed to confuse most players of guessing games: not mineral, not even vegetable as coal is, but animal. What a weird world... It should be taught in all schools – it was certainly taught in mine, back in the days when teachers usually had a free hand to sit back in their oaken chairs and waffle on about their special interests, to Hell with the prescribed curriculum, if there was one. I'd write all this to a newspaper except they wouldn't print it. Too old-fashioned.

We had a teacher, an old man who would have been retired if the war hadn't kept him on while all the younger staff had gone off to the War and not yet come back with their suede shoes and their limps ("Got it at Anzio, old man."). Mr Sewell was a little chap; we went to him for geography. In earlier days he had been a mountaineer, which seemed to us rather unlikely, so we used to encourage him to prove it. It was the weekly challenge, to turn whatever he was saying into a climbing reminiscence, and then tell him we found it hard to believe him. He would insist that he was telling the truth about his exploits, and it would end up with him demonstrating his prowess by climbing on top of the lockers, and from there circumnavigating the formroom, while we all applauded, without touching the floor. One day, when we was swaying on a tall bookcase about to swing across the door, the Headmaster came in. I have never seen such a masterly display of tact.

"Hello, Sewell, are you all right up there?"

"Thank you, Headmaster, yes."

"Well, carry on. This must have been tricky in Nepal, let me close the door so I can watch. Sit down, boys and learn… Oh, Sewell, see me later."

As you head towards the nice old town of Newport Pagnell, ignoring (I hope) the speedy but unutterably boring by-pass, there is a little hamlet called Chicheley, which I have always recognised as being the halfway point on my Bunny Run. The pub is right on the main road but I have never, not once, stopped there although you'd think it was an obvious place for a refresher. I ask myself: why not? It looks just as welcoming as any other. But, when I think about it, I realise that, very simply, human nature is at work. If you are keen to 'get on with things', your first target may well be the halfway point, but when you reach it, the unspoken urge is to make more progress: you press on, and stop off at a further point where you can relax in the knowledge that you are well into the second half. For me, that has always been in Newport Pagnell itself, over the hill and over the river…

But although I didn't stop, Chicheley was tantalising. Here was an apparently completely bereft hamlet: how could it have acquired its name? Any name?

Ekwall waffles on about possible owners' names but I think he is making most of it up: people he conjures up called Cicca or Cic… He eventually falls back exhausted on the most simple answer of all: "chicken-field". To me this seems not just completely obvious, but highly evocative: as people passed through, how better to describe the place? Who gave a damn what the landlord's name was, this was somewhere where you would find roosting hens and among the squawking fowl you may well discover, and walk away with, some eggs.

We need to look at the sideshows of history in the eyes of those who lived it. Judge it by their standards, not ours. That is the way to understand.

Sticking to the old main road, and refusing to be seduced by those enticing but utterly inhuman bypass signposts which nowadays lead the unwary into an interminable succession of soulless dual carriageways with numbers and ciphers instead of names, one eventually achieves Newport Pagnell. (But if you *have* been coaxed off, and on to the modern network, what bland horrors await you: the street layout in New York is bad enough – forty-ninth street west, and things like that – but at least they spell it out in words. Road number A.4.B. or whatever, is harsh and gruesome in the extreme).

Still on the old road, I went up the hill to the point where the weather changes. Have I told you about this? It is only a minor rise in the road, followed by a downward steep towards the river and the town; but time and again, over the years I have remarked upon rain or sunshine or snow stopping, or starting, at that point. This must be nothing less than the modest tail-end of the Pennines; and, our weather being what it is, it echoes in a minature way the behaviour of the clouds as, further north, they sweep in and pile up against the high hills – the spine of England – the way you can see from the air. If I were running that pub in Chicheley, I would change its name to 'The Coccyx'.

So: my next ancient bridge, at the foot of that hill; not easy to appreciate from the road but in a pleasant setting; and almost at once, another, and we reach Newport Pagnell. It must have been a river trading-post from early times, when the only serviceable road nearby, since Roman days, ran roughly south-north, while the Ouse slid smoothly west-east. It is already 'neuport' in Domesday, and in 1151 it was held by a gentleman called 'Pagellanus' which had become 'Pagnell' seventy years later. It would be good to know what happened to that family, and one day I must call in to the impressive-looking church and look for clues – though there will be a gap of a few hundred years, I expect, before official records start, so I'm probably out of luck. I wonder whether, as the top people of the parish, the Pagnells were themselves river-traders, sailing right down to The Wash and back; or did they merely charge a fee for access to the port, or perhaps rent out the craft? (A marketing suggestion for them: 'A boat for a groat'?)

As we enter the town we can begin at once to appreciate our wisdom in having ignored that dull and dreadful bypass. The old road right through to Watling Street, shows us a handful of ancient inns, a shop selling nothing but old magazines, a very nice little hotel full of Aston Martin executives and their well-heeled customers (but be careful if you're staying there overnight, as it's right next door to the church tower and the bells strike every fifteen minutes, or they did when I once tried it. Once only: do you know what it's like, all bloody night knowing that you have precisely fourteen minutes to get to sleep?); a couple of pleasant stop-offs alongside the meandering Grand Union Canal; a kennel with yelping hounds, opposite a lake; and eventually the well-concealed glamour of the still-used remains of one of our greatest railway works, full of the shades of those industrious Victorians and still surrounded by the crumbling memories of their off-duty hours – the tiny theatre, the street-corner pubs and chip shops, the site of the pawnshop and the Chapel; and eventually the almost-destroyed romance and glamour of the actual Roman highway, constantly in use for 1800 years.

Watling Street marches boldly out of London (nowadays from Marble Arch, which might have reminded the Romans of home though they would have thought it a bit puny!) and sweeps in a great curve up to Shrewsbury, after which it rather runs out of steam. I suppose the ruins of Wroxeter, or Uriconium, on the banks of the River Severn, mark some sort of terminus, or at least a junction, from which there were branches off to Chester to the north and all the Border stations southwards, as well as a rather less self-assured road venturing straight on towards Wales itself.

At the point where I hit Watling Street, it trudges in from the south as described by its villages: from Brickhill (old 'brig' meaning 'summit') to Bletchley (owned by a chap named 'Blecca', it says here); then we have Fenny Stratford, where the cohorts and their baggage-train would presumably wade warily through the marshy little tributary, the River Ouzel, one section at a time, and then gratefully dry off in the heat of trundling the next few miles until coming to my next favourite bridge: Stony Stratford. But in their day, you must remember, it was just as it says: a stony ford across the Ouse on their great Street.

I don't want to bore you with all this, but (as you know, I like to tell people things to put them right) I have just noticed one last interesting feature on the map hereabouts: we all know how industrious the Romans were, and we know this must have been an important staging-post for them, and no doubt therefore a trading centre to accommodate them since they must have been working up a thirst. So, look – two miles north and two miles south along Watling Street we find little places called Potsgrove and Pottersbury… Now, potteries don't move around because where they are situated is where their raw materials are. If there were people making pots in those hamlets around the time of Domesday, I reckon you could bet they had been there back in Roman times: whyever not?

Mind you, it was only another dozen miles up to the big town of Towcester (and have you heard American tourists trying to get that right?); so if our legion was marching north, once the ten cohorts had caught up and dried out, they might well have paused right here at Stony Stratford, and "dropped out for a smoke" as the Army saying is (if any of those Americans are reading this, that was a joke). Going in the other direction, though, it was a hell of a long way to Verulamium (St Albans, as it is now, named as it happens, after one of those Roman soldiers, who had, tragically for him, 'seen the light'), so perhaps they stayed the night and raised their elbows a few times with one of those local pots. I wonder what was in them.

I said just now, how the Ouse helpfully aided trade to the east and west. However, ten miles further south there was another crossroads, dry and well-trodden since ages before the Romans came. At or near Dunstable, high on the chalky Downs, that most ancient of all our trade-routes rolls across, its pedlars exchanging the tin and copper from the Cornish mines with the flint from Grimes Graves and similar spots of hard labour in East Anglia. The Ridgway with various name-changes by the locals ending with Peddar's Way (who was Peddar? Ekwall funks it), must have met Watling Street with a considerable clash of cultures? What a crossroads! I do hope somebody reliable is doing the digging...

And is 'Pedder' the same as 'pedlar'? Just a thought, for people more knowledgeable than I. Like you, who probably spotted this at once.

I would like you to notice my mastery of grammar. Recently, it seems to have become anarchically fashionable among the movers and shakers of our time, to ignore the rules, and use 'me' and 'I' indiscriminately. Two underlying influences have combined to spread this tendency to nearly everybody. First: television comedy shows have adopted and exaggerated the Queen's occasional phrase "My husband and I" without any reference to its context, nominative or accusative, and of course no grammatical background whatsoever. And secondly: our social-political commentators have cooked a great feast for themselves out of the selfish greed of those swindling in the City, loudly decrying the 'Me, Me, Me Generation'. So, 'I' is safer. Bring back, please, the teaching of Latin.

★★★

Enough of all this. I like to admire the constant survival of Watling Street but in particular the way it was, along the High Street at Stony Stratford, in later years. The heyday, the era of clattering hooves and trundling coaches. Not only for the Inns, the famous Cock and Bull amongst others, where the exchange of the latest rumours would be traded between coachmen, rogues and alarmists, to be conveyed to all parts of the country whether false or true; but also for the sad image of two small boys.

How does one warn small children to be untrusting?

It was around 1483; they were probably only half-aware that they were in the deepest peril, because nobody was telling them anything.

A great relief, when their kind uncle Richard had promised to take care of them, and arranged to have them met at an inn on this High Street.

One of the boys was the newly-inherited Duke of York, though he probably didn't understand it. The other was the King.

Shakespeare, a hundred years later, taking his cue from the perceptive Thomas More (who nevertheless lost his head), was pretty clear about what happened next; and it was a further two hundred years before two small skeletons were found under a staircase at the Tower of London.

What had gone through the minds of those bewildered children? Did they really trust Uncle Richard and his protection? Did they heave a sigh of relief as they welcomed his friendly staff, and were scooped up into the carriage and galloped down Watling Street to The Tower.

Children: be on your guard. Even when it is benevolent, you will be taken advantage of. Bad grammar, but so true.

ROUND THE DECK WITH MR HERTZOG

There was going to be a big event back at home, they had told him, and his Dad was expected to be part of it. A Coronation, in London. So they would be going back "on leave", from Mombasa down round the Cape. And then he would be staying in England at school. All very exciting...

He had few memories of their journey out three years ago, to Africa for the first time. Simply that he had been the only six-year-old on the boat, and the crew had jokingly made him run all the races for his age-group and then given him all the prizes: Winnie-the-Pooh, a jigsaw of the Mediterranean, and a stamp-album. And that he'd been suddenly and alarmingly kissed by some Baroness who had come aboard at Aden, and whom Dad called "Donner and Blitzen".

So, now this was the end of three splendid years in Nairobi. An uncomplicated and happy place for a youngster: you could cycle downtown with a pal any time, no need even to tell your parents – whyever should you? – everybody seemed friendly to everyone else, black, white or Indian. It would be nearly twenty years before people felt the alien need to sleep with a gun under the pillow...

★★★

He was accustomed to waking early, as school used to start at seven-thirty. So on the second day out, as the little British India ship chugged around the islands off Tanganyika on her way to a brief halt at Zanzibar, he started his routine of pacing round the decks soon after sunrise, and chatting to the sailors, of some unidentifiable exotic origin, while they hosed down the planks and spread out the deckchairs.

When they reached Durban and transferred to the big liner aiming for Southampton, he saw no reason to change his regime. The "Windsor Castle" was the last of the old-style Union Castle ships, with her four unfashionably tall funnels. She had been halfway through a complete refit, when the sudden demand for passages home resulted from the death of an old King and the abdication of the love-lorn next. The shipping line had hastily put back all the old fittings and plumbing, and steamed her frantically to Durban. All the cupboards rattled, but – as Mum generously allowed – the food was as good as ever; and what was more, this time he was eating with the grown-ups: at the Purser's table, too! Very swish.

But on his first early-morning outing on the big

new ship he found a few differences. The sailors sweeping the decks were no longer Madagascars or whatever it was his Dad had said, but English; well, British anyway. They smiled or said Hello, but didn't stop whatever it was they were doing: too busy, and there was always an officer of some sort keeping an eye on them. And he didn't even smile...

As on the smaller ship, though, no other passengers seemed to be up and about at that hour. Or so he thought until, turning to cross to the starboard side, he nearly bumped into a little old man with a hat on against the breeze, and walking with a stick. They both automatically said 'Sorry', stepped aside, and continued on their walks. A few yards further on, he passed two younger men who were in dark suits and not speaking to each other; but apart from that, he saw no passengers that morning. It wasn't very warm, so he only did the one round of the deck – and anyway, the decks were a much longer walk on this big Castle boat.

The rest of the day was spent just mooching about, exploring the facilities like the gym, the swimming-pools and the library; or hanging over the rail watching the sea go past. But there were two ports of call before Capetown – East London and Port Elizabeth – and they both provided some excitement. At one, because she was so big, the ship had to anchor offshore and passengers were lowered over the side in a huge basket into a launch; at the other, there was a snake-park with a famous man called Johannes who walked in among them, deadly though they were, and draped them around himself. He made a lot of money from tourists but I think the snakes won in the end.

***

The early morning walks had continued during this erratic journey, but he had been entirely alone, so far as fellow passengers were concerned. However, the next morning they were heading North at last out of Capetown, where they had sensationally taken the cable car up to the top of Table Mountain, doing the trip early to avoid the "table-cloth" of cloud that so often gathers in the afternoon: using the telescope, he had been able to identify their cabin on the ship in the harbour…

Now, all of a sudden, and again as he rounded the deck towards the stern, he met the little wizened man with the floppy hat and the walking-stick. They smiled at each other.

"Good morning, young man."

"Good morning, sir. I thought you had disembarked," the boy said – he had picked up the word and was keen to use it.

"Ah. I had business in Durban, so I came up to Capetown by train."

Up, to Capetown? On the map it was 'down'?

The two grey men, still in suits, came round the corner.

"Well, we'll meet again, I'm sure: it's more than a week to England". He moved on with another smile. The two men still weren't talking to each other.

***

The next morning he brushed his hair first thing, and took his comb with him in case of strong winds. They met halfway along the port side, so they had seen each other approaching and the old man had had time to think. He stopped, and so did the two men a few yards behind, who looked a bit foolish and fidgetted.

"Isn't it a bit lonely, my lad? I quite like being alone with my thoughts but I do that the rest of the day. Why not do an about turn and walk along with me?" He turned, for the first time, to the suits. "That's all right, isn't it?"

They muttered to each other, then shrugged and nodded.

"These security men," he confided to the boy as they walked on, "have no conversation, none at all. I could be walking with wildebeests."

As you would expect, most of their talk was made up of the old man asking the boy about his life and his interests. They dealt with school lessons, teachers good and bad, sports days, hobbies… It emerged that they both had quite good collections of British Empire stamps, and the boy confided that he had once seen a Mauritius Post Office Penny Red. (The old man had once actually owned one, but he didn't say so).

"Have you ever been to Mauritius, sir? It's over there somewhere, I think," waving a hand seaward.

"Well, remember we're round the Cape now, so actually it's over that way, back in the Indian Ocean where we were when we first met. Where you are pointing, it's Ascension Island; now, they've got some good stamps. I have been there, once upon a time."

"Do you go to lots of places on business?"

"Quite a bit, I did, but I think it's all over now."

It sounded like a slight sigh, and they didn't talk much more for a while. For a couple of minutes they stopped and leaned over the rail. The ship was going through a huge flotilla of enormous jellyfish, in all sorts of pastel shades, blue, pink, yellow. Like dinner-plates, the boy said. Like dustbin-lids, the old man suggested.

"Don't try collecting *them*," he added, "some can give a terrible sting. A shock, really – it can kill you."

"And yet they look so pretty and harmless."

"There's certainly a moral there. Things are not as they seem," he muttered more or less to himself as they walked on, "But people won't thank you for proving it." They came to the gangway where their paths parted. "See you tomorrow," and he waved his stick.

★★★

Next day they were keeping close to the coastline of what must by now have been the diamond coast of South West Africa, where access by land was reputedly almost impossible and the shores were littered with gemstones. It didn't look much like that.

However, they found an excitement over to starboard: the wreck of a ship; a ship, fairly recent, up against a rock. Abandoned obviously and looking very sorry for herself. You could make out her name: the Something-or-Other 'Maru'. So, the old man said, she was Japanese. He wondered what had happened.

"Would it have been in the War, sir, like that wreck outside the harbour in Zanzibar?"

"No, no, it's not been there long. But I well remember the Zanzibar sinking."

"Were you in the War?"

"Not the 14-18, no. But I was in the Boer War."

"My Grandad was in that," the boy announced proudly, and he saw the rise of a sardonic eyebrow. "He was in the Cavalry: the Ninth Lancers."

"We fought them at Modder River."

The boy gasped, but tried to hide it with a cough. He was talking to the enemy!

It came as a relief to get to the gangway. They parted with the usual smile, well, almost; and even the two suits managed to twist their lips in an effort to be sociable. But it had been a disturbing moment. He thought he'd better check back with his parents.

★★★

The Purser had devised a seating rota at his dinner-table, more for his own relief than that of his guests, one would imagine; and this evening the boy found himself placed right next to that Officer, with Mum and Dad variously opposite. Chat with the Purser was a bit like that first walk round the deck: school, teachers good and bad (but toned down a bit as Mum and Dad were keenly listening to judge his conversational skills). When they had dealt with sports days and hobbies, and the fruit and cheeses had arrived at the table, he decided to demonstrate his savoir-faire.

"Actually," he told everybody, "I have made friends with an old gentleman up on deck. I see him every morning and we walk around together."

"Really," said his Mum. "Who is he?"

"I don't know yet, but he's very nice, even though he's a Boer left over from the Boer War."

The Purser had dropped a slice of cheese and was sitting forward.

"I haven't seen him anywhere else on board, ever. I think he stays in his cabin with his two other friends, I've never seen him here for meals."

Mum and Dad had become protective and anxious and wanted to know what the old man had been saying, doing, acting strange. Had he touched him or anything? But the Purser was far more practical. Did he have a walking-stick? Did he always have two security bodyguards who were a bit – what can I say – taciturn?

"Yes, sir, absolutely."

The Purser asked and obtained permission to pour the boy a watery half-glass of something special that was on the table. "Your boy," he said, "Has the unique distinction of making a friend of the South African Prime Minister, Hertzog."

Gasps all round.

"He keeps to himself all day," the Purser enlarged, "but goes round the deck for a constitutional very early in the morning. He is travelling to England, like so many officials, for the Coronation, and wants to remain incognito. So hearty congratulations my boy, but –" to the whole table, "confidences, please. No mention of this."

For the next few mornings, the strolls continued,

and their chats were wide-ranging. At last the boy had persuaded the old man to talk about events at the turn of the century, and he listened enthralled. He did however notice an increasing number of early risers doing the round of the deck, or at least part of it, or at worst looking out of the doors and windows. This was also observed by the two suits, who began to walk much closer and whose eyes seemed to swivel like something out of a George Raft movie, or maybe that new man Peter Lorre, however you pronounced it.

After that, and just before they called at Madeira, the old man said to him, as they leant on the rail and watched whales blowing in the distance: "I'm sorry, son, but I won't be seeing you after today. I'm told I can't walk round any more as we've been doing."

The boy looked sad at this, but said: "I understand that, sir. You see, I know who you are. It must be very difficult for you, being Prime Minister and all that. But please, Mr Hertzog, just please wait here for a minute, I'd like to have your autograph. Could I? I'll go and fetch my new book, I only bought it in Capetown."

The bodyguards didn't seem to object, they were even smiling, unheard of…

He was back in a minute.

"Leave it with me," said the old man, "and I'll do it as soon as I get back to my cabin where my best pen is. The pen I've signed all those War Treaties with."

* * *

In fact, the next day was taken up with a visit to Madeira

and a trip on some sort of ox-drawn sleigh to the top of some mountain or other that the locals were very proud about; though the chief memory was of crowds of tiny boats which came up alongside and held up masses of lace: curtains, table-cloths, dresses, Heaven knows what, but he photographed it all. It was in the evening that the package came.

It was hand-addressed and inside was his autograph book.

A covering note said: "Dear Lad, This is in memory of a delightful though brief relationship which has greatly eased my recent burdens. Good luck to you." (He hadn't signed it). But there was a PS "When you get to your new school in England, though you will feel lonely at first, the enclosed may help you to make friends with similarly-minded collectors."

He opened the autograph album. Right the way through, it was signed on every recto page: "J B M Hertzog, PM." There must have been a hundred of them.

* * *

He never met the old man again. He always fondly remembered him with his slanted hat, his walking-stick, and the way he toddled around the deck, one hand always deeply in his coat pocket. And, just think, he had been the confidant of a Prime Minister…?

As they docked at Southampton, with his parents, they passed the waiting time by leaning over the rail and watching the VIPs going down the gangplank. So this was The Old Country he had more than half forgotten out there where the sun shone seriously with the

altitude calming it down to a Spring day. He had loved Kenya.
There was a slight commotion. An unrecognised elderly man was chaperoned down to the quay, at once surrounded by jobsworths and journalists. The Purser was passing by. He said: "Did he say a proper goodbye to you?"

"Who?"

"That's Hertzog."

"But – ."

"Didn't you say you walked round the deck together? That's not him? Good God, which deck?"

It rapidly became clear that JBM Hertzog, Prime Minister, Boer War General, out-and-out achiever, hero of his country, had spent the early mornings getting his exercise on the upper deck of the Windsor Castle, that exclusive one where all the real toffs hung out. But in that case – .

His question was answered, as his own friendly old man was led down the gangplank a few minutes later by two grey men in suits. His right hand held that walking-stick; his left was now out of its pocket and handcuffed to Suit Number One, who still wasn't smiling much. All that exercise on the lower deck had done little for him.

The boy turned to the Purser for help.

"Arrested in Durban, taken for a hearing in Capetown, and now he's brought back to London for trial. Fraud and forgery. But his age may help him. After all, a well-known figure in the Boer War although he never got any recognition. No, no family."

"He'll get recognition now," the boy said. And as

soon as he arrived at his new school he joined the History Club; he sold all those autographs of Hertzog at two shillings a time.

But he doesn't go to their reunions very often – he remembers the moral of the pretty jellyfish.

VI

The road to Lesson One

I really did walk round the deck early every morning, with the real Prime Minister Hertzog, in 1937, though at the age of nine I had no idea that he was somebody important. So far as I can remember, there were no spooks shadowing us – life wasn't that dangerous; I didn't think to ask for his autograph: whyever should I? But anyway, I was on the right deck. The rest of it I made up, just a few weeks ago, so you are the first to know. It makes a better story, doesn't it ?

It was too soon to ring my home number again: it would take my wife's brother a good half-hour to get there, and I was pretty sure he would await my call. So I drove down that short stretch of the Roman road that is now the High Street of Stony Stratford and pulled up for a quick refresher at either the Cock or the Bull, I couldn't tell which as it was dark and it hardly mattered: I just needed a quick one.

I took the local OS map in with me, as I usually do wherever I go; and was surprised to see that Milton Keynes is surrounded by water. Lakes and ponds all over the place, and the little Ouzel winding through to join its big brother back in Mr Pagnell's land. Another surprise is that this is a recent name for the tributary: until the mid 1800s it was apparently, Mr Ekwall says, known as the Whizzle Brook, meaning 'weasel' and then this evolved into 'Ouzel' due to the larger river. I don't know how the 'z' got into it unless it's because slow-flowing rivers do, I suppose, 'ooze'...

The names of settlements large or small, as I have said, are decided by the locals or people visiting them, tax-collectors in particular. But nobody has ever attempted to tax a river, so far as I know, and this lack of interference or repeated recording has meant that our river names have changed very little, many of them dating right back to before the Romans, let alone the incoming Anglo-Saxons. Caesar wrote of the Tamesis in 51 BC; in 150 AD the Tyne was Tina and the Exe was Iska. The ancient Britons, up and down the country, and utterly remote from each other unless they were in the tin or flint trade, would naturally use their simple general words to describe the local watercourse on which they depended. For instance, our old friend Eilert reckons that Tame, Tamar, Teme, Teign and Thames may have been from a word for 'dark water'; apparently the Eden, up in Cumbria, comes from a root meaning 'gushing forth' but how he knows that surely deserves a book of its own! Disappointingly, my lovely Ouse (and the namesake up in Yorkshire) just means 'water'. So does Avon, and there are several of those. There is a small river up in Northumberland called the Breamish which Ekwall says means 'roaring' and one day I must go and listen to it. At the other extreme, he lists three rivers called the Idle, and he can't decide whether it means just that, or 'shining and bright'. I would like to think it meant both and I would like to picnic beside any of them.

Once across the Watling Street bridge, where the legion would have waded over the stony ford, cursing the British for their cold weather, and if they were heading north for a warlike reason, maybe throwing a sestertius into the stream for good luck from their gods, I turned left towards Buckingham. The road stays close to the Ouse, which almost visibly shrinks as it grows younger: but even at the end of this stretch it still behaves itself: true enough, though I hate to admit it, it oozes.

I told you as we first met the river, back in St. Neots, that it would dwindle to 'an old man's jump', and I have just wondered how many old men might have had to jump across the river along this stretch, or perhaps made use of a fallen treetrunk, before somebody on a local Council took pity: there are a host of side-roads off to the left, seeking out the secret hamlet bordering the river, and today each of them enjoys a modest single-span bridge. Some are hump-backed like that infamous one now marked for posterity by my old Aunt Doris; these bridges were designed centuries ago for a flock of dithering sheep or the occasional creaking ox-cart; but now they are 'improved' to take not only the bulging milk lorry but the mock-modest gynaecological shrieks of teenaged girls as they are driven fast over it by the farmer's son. I wonder who was the first young man to discover this subtle shortcut to a successful rural courtship – and was it the man or the girl, I ask myself with a cynical eyebrow...

Apart from those tempting side-turnings, it is an

uneventful road, and I have never found anything along it to tell you about; so I switched on the car radio, stuck as always, and to my great joy there was the tail-end of a concert. I had been just in time to catch the end of something by that extraordinary survivor, the almost-centenarian Francois-Joseph Gossec. The fact that he churned out thirty symphonies, twenty operas, and a Te Deum requiring fifteen hundred players, is largely beside the point: look at his dates. Imagine yourself as a musician and composer, living through such an era and its upheavals in the bedrock of popular music…

He had been born in 1734 when the Bach family were just getting their act together: the great Johann Sebastian was in his prime and was about to walk 200 miles to hear Buxtehude play the organ; he was about seven when Handel, after a stroke, produced The Messiah in a fortnight; a few years after that he was being taught by Rameau, who had been born when we still had Charles II on the throne, and who himself had been a pupil of Lully, who was also a dancing master at the French court and had died after stabbing himself in the foot with his beating-time staff… Gossec plodded quietly on, as good Belgians do. He was a boy chorister at Antwerp but, as for composing his own stuff, he largely taught himself: Rameau died in 1764 when Gossec was thirty, and a pushy young Austrian called Mozart was giving concerts of his own work at the age of eight. Brilliant, as we all know, with that mystical touch that could create pure magic even with one piano-note at a time like in No 21's slow movement, he was either too pushy or too far ahead, and alas dead and buried (somewhere?) in 1791, while Gossec was modestly putting on operas in Paris, and teaching composition to reluctant students at the Conservatoire. Not only Mozart and Weber came and went; Weber was born when our quiet hero was over 50, he burnt out forty brilliant years later, and Gossec still had three years to go. He saw off young Schubert, too... When he was born, remember it was Handel and the Bachs; when he died, Chopin and Liszt were touring Europe, Wagner was full of teenage Rhine-maiden dreams, and both Johann Strauss and Offenbach were up and running...

Only a few closing minutes, then we were back to the residual nonsense of the modern Radio Three where the current planning seems to insist that, once those of us who enjoy anything tuneful have been pacified for a couple of hours, the rest of the day must be devoted to the needs of the minorities; and the tinier the minority, the more airtime it must be given. On this day, somebody just back from Kisumu was going to tell us gasping listeners all about the songs they were singing in the forests, in the original local Swahili sub-dialect, never before recorded. Never again, either, I told myself as I tried to change channels; but no.

And why do folk songs always have too many verses?

★★★

The tall slender spire of Buckingham church showed up in daytime, heartening against the sky and this time I simply had to imagine it in the darkness. It is a welcoming little town, and these days I ignore the boring new bypass with its endless roundabouts, and still go through the centre, with the chocolate-box gaol right in the middle of the market-place, presumably where it was most needed, and a convenience for the constabulary?

The church stands proud on the highest point, hovering above the little Ouse, and strongly hinting that it might have been sited on top of an earlier, pre-Christian fortification: those British or post-Roman hillforts weren't all as spectacular as the famous examples at Cadbury or Caradoc. If you happened to live in a place without high land around it, it was still just as necessary – maybe more so – to devise some protection for your family, your animals and your livelihood. Alongside a wide stream, so much the better.

Hundreds of years later, with an organised social order and the times less individually nervous, you would have been persuaded that both your fears and your protection came from God. This was the message from both the local priest and his patron the landlord. There was nobody else to turn to: and you were threatened with Hell one way or the other by both of them.

It must therefore have seemed obvious to position one's fine new church as the pinnacle of the town. Often there may be a surround of the old pagan earthworks (look for churches where the churchyard is oval or circular), where the old gods have been demonstrably crushed under the One True God. Psychology and PR go back a long way.

The landlord, I suppose though I haven't yet done any

research, was presumably the Duke – at least somewhere along the line, though no doubt he lived rather nearer to the Court and seldom, if ever, visited the source of his wealth. The first Duke, round about 1600, became a rather-too-close friend, a bosom pal one has to say, of the *nouveau-anglais* King James the First, who was apparently besotted with him, calling his acolyte 'Steenie' which can't have helped either much. Steenie was rather messily removed from the scene after James's death by a man called Felton, unknown to us for any other contribution to the nation's wellbeing, since he was rather promptly executed for the deed. The next Duke compensated for all this by being a prominent politician and member of the Cabal under Charles II. And after him, the third Duke bought a rather large house which had been built on a mulberry garden at the end of The Mall and technically in Pimlico…

You know how, when you are driving along at night, all sorts of disconnected thoughts flow through? Two of them have just done this to me. First: nobody knows where the district known as Pimlico got its name from: it is first recorded as the name of a special brew of beer in 1598. Then, even the Oxford University Press seems to go haywire: its Dictionary says, in my 1972 edition, that the word describes an Australian bird 'from the sound it makes', first recorded in 1848. But the OUP's Companion to English Literature in my 1975 (reprinted with corrections) tells us that it is indeed a bird but West Indian, and first recorded back in 1614. More corrections pending? And how the hell can any bird say "Pimlico" unless it's some sort of parrot? More research needed.

The other thought that occurred to me, was that James I is given rather a rough time by most of today's historians, who sneer at his pretty-obvious homosexuality and his physical disabilities (apparently he dribbled and drooled all the time). OK, no Adonis, but first let's look at his background. His mother, Mary Queen of Scots, was involved in a succession of murders, plots and assassinations, which can't have made for a really happy childhood; and then she was imprisoned throughout his most impressionable years, having married three times which surely didn't help young James? When he succeeded to our throne in 1603, life wasn't much more secure: witness the Gunpowder Plot. Yet, aside from his weakness and personal proclivities, he wrote a number of very powerful treatises, the most famous being the criticism of Tobacco, now fully justified after four hundred years. Above all, he ordered and promoted the Authorised Version of the Bible, that great poem which has become perhaps the most splendid example of the English language as it was, still is when permitted, and for ever should be. James, we undervalue you still.

Through Buckingham then, I pick up the road to Bicester, and begin to think about the Army. Ten miles ahead of me is the sprawling Ordnance Depot which I remember from my own National Service years; but long before that, on a downhill bend in my road just after the village of Tingewick (come on, Ekwall?) there is an overgrown turning off to the right, where I remember a barrier and a Nissen-hut guardroom in the 1950s. This must have been an Army Camp of some sort, as there were uniformed people moving about when I drove past. But now it has all been utterly demolished. Has this elimination of war memories taken place all over the country? I suppose, unless forbidden, all the local farmers will have done their best to reclaim their commandeered land. It is understandable. An airfield for bombers would have absorbed many acres of potential celery or potato or other East Anglian crops; and further inland, training camps or storage centres would have been quickly reclaimed, to be sure.

But that little memory would always spark off in my mind a thought about the crafty conscripted opportunists who contrived to make National Service worthwhile. It was tempting to imagine a clerk in Company Office managing to 'create' an intake of perhaps several dozen recruits, think up names and backgrounds for them, then sneak them on to the payroll… I was going to write a play about this but my fiction was overtaken by reality: some clever chaps really did it!

So, instead, I talked to my Grandad. He told me about his time as a regular in the Ninth Lancers. And about the day he first joined.

Here it is.

LESSON ONE

Nothing much had been happening in Cornwall that year, my grandfather used to tell us; and that was why he'd gone off to join the Army. It was 1894 and he was seventeen – perhaps a bit young for his age, but he was a well-set-up youngster and keen to see the world. I remember him saying, too, how that year was the first time he'd seen one of the new sixpences showing the Queen as a really old lady, and somehow this had shaken him (and, I suppose, many people in the far ends of the country) and given him a sense of the passing of time and an urgency to be up and doing...

He knew a bit about horses, which wasn't unusual in those days I know, but he'd worked around the local stables and his uncle was a blacksmith and so on. (I still remember how, years and years later when he was old and retired, he used to groom us before Sunday School: sweeping us down with the coat-brush in the hall, and puffing out his breath as hard as he could to keep the dust away – Poooooof like that – the same as he'd been taught to do with the horses in the old days).

So this was why he found himself in Canterbury, picking his way across the cobbles from the railway station on his journey to the Cavalry Barracks, half excited, half terrified, with all his belongings in a very small brand-new attaché-case. It was a hot day and I reckon he could smell his way to the Barracks without much need to ask directions; reaching the gate, he headed for the Guard Room and fished in his pocket for the papers he had to present on reporting. First, he paused in the sunshine and gathered his nerves together, admiring the blue sky and sniffing the warm horsey air...

"YOU THERE!!" It came like a screech-owl into a dream – the voice seemed to echo from everywhere and he looked around wildly at this first taste of the parade-ground. Strutting towards him across the square, covered in stripes and insignia and braid, was a surprisingly small but immensely smart Sergeant Major, with a pair of beady eyes just visible below the rim of his immaculate cap. The eyes were not smiling… The sinister little moustache, however, was twitching as he marched – and twitching in step, which was perhaps the most unnerving thing.

So far as my grandfather thought at all at that moment, he thought that here was somebody who had just been through the First Boer War and couldn't wait for the next one… He knew he must stand still, and very upright: he did so.

"STAND STILL!!" said the screech-owl. "STAND UPRIGHT!!"

He drew himself together even more, so that he could scarcely breathe – though indeed for the moment he had stopped breathing anyway.

"Boy!" shouted the Sergeant-Major, stamping to attention beside him and lowering the trajectory of his voice not very much, "have you got some silly idea of joining this Regiment?"

The recruit stammered without saying anything.

"Lesson One," said the apparition. "You cannot be of service to your country with your hands in your pockets. I tell you once. Understood?"

The young man pulled the documents from his pocket and held them out, but the Sergeant-Major ignored them majestically. "In the Squadron Office you'll find the Duty Sergeant. Report there, boy, and I don't want any trouble with you again".

"Yes sir," said the recruit. "Sorry, sir."

"I'M NOT *SIR*," came the screech. "I'M SAR'MAJOR. OFFICERS IS *SIR*. That's Lesson One… I tell you once."

The beady eyes flicked quickly up and down in a well-practised scanning of the body before him. "It seems to me," he shouted thoughtfully, "we have here all the makings of a very poor soldier. Oh dear me yes…" and he spun on his glinting heel and marched away, at the twitch.

★★★

I imagine the rest of that day was the usual routine for a new recruit: filling in forms, medical examinations, and all the rest. There was always a gap in my grandfather's story at this point, since his encounter at the gate so paralysed him, nothing that followed was clear until the evening… But then he had crossed from the cook-house, where he'd passed an unhappy half-hour with a most *un*-Cornish-farmhouse tea, and found his way to his bed, down the far end of a long and alien barrack-room.

He sat down wearily, as we all must have done after our first bewildering military day; and he looked around the room at the rows of disciplined beds and cupboards belonging to "Them" – the old hands, the seasoned Troopers as he saw them, who had been through it all and survived and were now the smug possessors of tattered pay-books, hardened muscles, smooth boots – local girl-friends even, they might be walking out with… Nobody had spoken to him today… He counted the beds, and wondered how many others like him had stayed here briefly, and then failed to make the grade. That was the side of things you didn't hear about from the recruiting officer.

Suddenly in a panic he remembered that he had to report to the Quartermaster's Stores to get "kitted out"... He had almost left it too late. All day still in his civvies, now was the time they'd told him to attend the important ritual of receiving one's uniform and equipment, ready for parade at first light tomorrow.

He ran out of the barrack-room and across the square...

"YOU THERE!!" The nightmare was back, as the terrible Sergeant Major bore down upon him, all-seeing, omnipresent. "Oh dear oh dear," he murmured to himself thunderously, "what a very poor soldier this is going to be... Boy," he went on, "what is Lesson One?

"Lesson One as every *good* soldier knows," he continued with hardly a breath, "is that you will not run you will *walk* when crossing the parade-ground is that understood I tell you once oh my goodness a very useless little soldier."

The Sergeant Major gathered himself up into his whirlwind and spun away.

Over at the stores, the Squadron Quarter-Master Sergeant issued a parade uniform, a best uniform, a stable dress to wear on fatigues, some first boots, some second boots, a pill-box cap, a forage cap, lots of underwear, a bagful of equipment all to be polished by morning, a buttonstick, a hairbrush marked WD, a Bible, a tooth-brush and a huge cut-throat razor which was something quite outside the boy's experience... All this was signed for, wrapped inside three grey blankets also marked WD, and he staggered back with it to his bed.

The aged Corporal in charge of the hut, and one or two of the other men, exchanged a few words with him during the evening, but he was in no mood to talk anyway... He made his bed, he polished, he stared glumly at all the weird property of Her Majesty for which he had signed his name, he polished some more; and eventually he climbed into bed and in the dark he lay there quietly wishing he wasn't too old to cry himself to sleep.

He was going to be a useless little soldier: he had been told so twice already, and by an expert.

⋆⋆⋆

In the morning however, he found his courage returned. Reveille came as no shock to him – it was only a bugle instead of a cockerel. Amid the coughs and curses of his mates he got himself ready for the mysteries of the day – he dressed as they dressed, tidied and folded as they tidied and folded, watching them out of the corner of his eye... In ones and twos they disappeared into the wilderness of the wash-house which was somehow disgusting in its very fluid cleanliness; and they finally emerged into the open air smelling of carbolic and transformed into cavalrymen.

He was last on parade, but only by half-a-minute, and as he lined up for inspection he felt for the first time a twinge of pride in himself as a soldier: first time in uniform, he was well-polished, well-washed, he was standing to attention with the rest of them, he was going to be a credit to his Squadron... In time, a credit to the Regiment... In time –

Slowly down the ranks towards him came the inspection. But it wasn't just the young inoffensive NCO who had called them on parade! – Moustache all a-tremble, eyes flickering like a fly in a jam-jar, approached the dreaded Sergeant Major. His gospel radiated all around him, an aura of shine and polish which proclaimed that these were *his* men, whom he had created out of Chaos, out of the dismal dust that had drifted over the years into his barracks. His to form, his to destroy... And in these men his Troopers – most of them – he was well-pleased: you could catch now and then a grunt of his satisfaction as he came nearer... "Good man... good... hair-cut! ... good man..."

From time to time the words were lost in the clatter as a troop of exercising cavalry went past; but then at last the Sergeant Major came to a halt in front of the new recruit, and the stony eyes squinted under their cap as they performed their tour of his uniform, his boots, his face... And at the face they hardened, narrowed into a closer scrutiny.

"Well boy, didn't they kit you out last night?"

"Yes sir – yes, sarn't-major."

"You've forgotten something then?" The voice was on a higher pitch and now there was an edge to it... The Sergeant Major grew red around the neck. "Got no razor, then, haven't you boy?"

So that was it! Of all the things he had tried so hard to do correctly this morning, he had forgotten the obvious one which would have placed him among the men – and here he was, exposed as a useless boy… He had never shaved in his life; the down on his chin had never needed attention, and he thought of his new razor, if at all, as something for use vaguely in the future. There was nothing he could say without making himself ridiculous; weakly he admitted that Yes, sarn't-major, he had a razor…

"What's it for, boy, what's it for? Fall out, smart now, and shave your bottom lip proper. Report back to me in twenty minutes – MOVE!!"

★★★

Back in the barrack-room he sat on the edge of his bed in the depth of despair, and stared at the razor – a vicious instrument of bright steel and artificial mother-of-pearl which the Queen had lent him yesterday… He hadn't the faintest idea what to do with it. When it opened he scared himself with the gruesome possibilities that flooded into his miserable head…

"What's up, lad?" It was the old Corporal, off duty and resting across the room: old as the hills he really was, white-haired with a ruddy face tanned by all the winds and sands of the Khyber and Khartoum. He was the nearest thing to a Chelsea Pensioner you could still find on the payroll, the men used to say. God knows why he was still around, but the Depot made good use of him to fetch and carry, and as the Regiment was his life, it was a workable arrangement… He got up and came over, sitting down beside the boy and taking the razor from him.

A kind face, in a strange place… There ought to be

a saying about it. Anyway, out tumbled the whole story: the shaving problem, the useless soldier problem, and over and above it all the terror and the despair brought about by that creature of the devil, the Sergeant Major who was more than God, who despised this green newcomer but would have all the powers of life and death over him for perhaps twenty years.

"Well," said the Corporal, going for some hot water, "we've only ten minutes to go, so we'd better get on with it. Yes, I'll give you a shave, and then tonight we can practise so you know how it's done. After all," he wagged his finger, "if you're going to soldier on, you've got to learn; if you're going to run away, you'd better look respectable; and if you're going to cut your throat we've got to ship you home in good condition... So sit you down and we'll get started."

As he bubbled the lather, he said: "You know, you mustn't get too worried about these sergeants and warrant officers... It's just a job they're doing... The shouting and the yelling's what they get paid for..."

The boy protested at this, but got soap in his mouth. He just sat and listened, while the red face and its purple veins and the framework of white hair blurred into a sort of close-up, molten Union Jack as the razor scraped away.

"Now, take our Sergeant Major," the old man went on, "he raves away on parade like a Bashi-Bazouk and he scares the daylights out of everybody; but I'll tell you this – I remember him when he first joined the Regiment – even then I was a Corporal – and he was a young lad like you, but d'you know, he couldn't even get on a horse! And something else: he's got a family of his own now, and a couple of boys, and they love him. Love him, they do."

This all sounded most improbable, but in view of the razor the boy couldn't say anything without a serious risk of bloodshed.

"You'll find out soon enough, lad, that our sarn't-major is as human as the next man... Mark my words, you'll find out real soon..." Chuckling away, we wiped the blade and stood back.

"There," he said, "now you're all Sir-Garnet. Run off back on parade and report for inspection... But remember, you've done the job for yourself – whatever you do, don't let on I helped you, that'd be a big mistake."

⋆⋆⋆

Supper that night was pretty good, and it was quite late when the boy got back to the barrack-room with some of his mates. They laughed a bit at the old Corporal, who was already in bed and looking more than ever like a Chelsea Pensioner. But later on he went over to thank the old man.

"How did it go?"

"It's all thanks to you, Corp. Sarn't-major said it was much better, a real improvement; he said I looked real smart now."

The Corporal twinkled, "Made all the difference, did it?"

"He really smiled at me, Corp.; he said I'd got the

makings of a real good Trooper," the boy told him proudly. The old red-white-and-blue face flapped with laughter. "A big improvement! See what I mean, lad, about him being human? When I shaved you this morning I was using the wrong side of the razor!"

He sat up in the bed and wiped his eyes. "They may behave like God's elder brother, but they're only human after all. That's Lesson One," he said, "*that's* Lesson One."

VII

The road to Hay Mill

I think most of us underestimate our grandparents. I know I did. That story is absolutely as he told it to me: completely true. But already, by the time he arrived at that depot, he had gone through some unusual experiences. His grandparents were rooted in the soil of East Cornwall, to be sure, at a small village called Duloe, south of Liskeard and just before you get to the rocky sea at Looe. But his Dad had followed the general drift towards the towns in the mid-Victorian years, and joined the Royal Navy at Plymouth, not far away.

He had spent his life as a leading stoker, in some of the first warships to run on coal; and Grandad had been born and brought up in Torpoint (and would tell us endlessly about "The Hole In The Wall" through which you had to look when walking down to the ferry in order to check the timing of the departure from Devonport). Yes, that was typical grandparent-boredom; but if you went on listening, you could pick up a lot more...

He decided to follow his Dad into the Navy; and soon found himself as a recruit seaman at Greenwich. I think this must mean that he had been identified as meriting promotion, what we later called "Officer potential", and I say this only because that was what happened at Greenwich in the early 1890s. He went there with a friend from home in Torpoint, whose name I have somewhere...

There is a photo of dozens of these naval recruits up aloft, standing (terrified?) along the yard-arms or whatever they are called, having shinned up on ropes, and proved themselves to be whatever it was they were expected to be... He once indicated to me, which one he was. I was too much of a young fool to mark it on the photo, so now his presence fifty feet up, swaying above the waves for his country, is lost forever.

Unfortunately for his Royal Naval ambitions, both he and his friend became rather quickly disenchanted. It wasn't until Grandad was in his seventies, that he unburdened himself to me (and I don't think he ever told my father, his only son, because one simply didn't talk about such things, to anyone, in the pre-war days). Once installed at Greenwich, their country innocence was shattered, at a stroke by the sexual attentions of their long-service-and-good-conduct Bo'sun – or whatever he was called – who was in absolute charge of them...

In short, they ran away. OK, they deserted... But rather than cause a fuss around 1890 by reporting it, they just went and joined the Army instead, Grandad into the Ninth Lancers and his friend into a Hussar regiment, I don't know which... After all, from life at home they were more familiar with farm horses than sea-horses.

There is a curious coda to this. Grandad rose to be the Regimental Quartermaster Sergeant in the Ninth in the

Boer War, and after it he joined the Civil Service; but in 1914 he was recalled, given a commission and put in charge of Indian pioneers because he spoke their language… Then demobilised in 1918 he became a library assistant in the House of Lords Library, a fascinating job where he chatted with all sorts of important people and used to get trout, grouse, pheasants or partridge to take home on the Southern Railway almost every appropriate month. In the middle of all this, in the 1930s, he was suddenly visited in the Lords Library by two men accusing him of desertion from the Navy! Of course, he was completely cleared and vindicated; but what an example of the slow grinding of the mills of bureaucracy! The Bo'sun must have been dead for years; Grandad was heavy with medals (I once counted eight) and had served King and Country blamelessly for some forty years. One wonders who was the jobsworth at the Admiralty with nothing better to do, although no doubt "The Fleet was Lit Up".

As I've said, the dozen miles to Bicester are uneventful except that you could open up at various points once upon a time and go well over 100 so long as you knew nothing was coming out of the side-roads, and it was a decent morning. But once you hit the little town itself, nostalgia cut in… You knew that you were entering the aura of that crowd of busy Roman wives and children of 1800 years ago… I often tried to make comparisons between them and their successors at today's sprawling Ordnance Depot, covering with their shopping-lists exactly the same ground, buying very much the same foods, while their men were being bullied on their parade-ground by exactly the same type of power-crazy junior NCOs.

But what were the Romans' imported delicacies? A book called *'Roman Panorama'* (1944) by my old Headmaster Humfrey Grose-Hodge has pages about this: they would have brought in wine, of course, no doubt about that; but garlic and olive oil would have been much in demand. They would have found a few common fruits in our hedgerows and have put up with them because Mediterranean produce could not saleably have travelled so far: but they did introduce cherries. The most pleasing fact, to me, is the edible snail population. In a ditch in the Cotswolds is a colony of them, descendants of the ones they brought in, all that time ago; less than a hundred yards away are the ruins of the Roman Villa. A slow rate of travel indeed, but why travel when you are left well alone and you're happy where you are? I do hope it stays like that for them, after this discovery.

To judge by the great heaps of them at prehistoric sites, I guess we already knew about shellfish: and apparently the Romans weren't all that keen on fish, back home; yet I'll bet they soon had to get used to it when they were stationed around our coasts. As for animals, I expect they brought in their own. And did someone tell me they introduced rabbits to us, or was that the Normans? The word appears to come from Northern French: it is 'robbet' in Belgium, or 'robbe', back in the Middle Ages, though in France today it's 'lapin', and where did that come from? I'm told that 'rabbit' in olden times was only the young animal: was there a word 'robb' for the mature one, leaving off the diminutive? But there was a different word for the grown-up: the word 'cony'... And ah! Now we are getting somewhere: the word 'cony' derives from the improbable Latin: 'cuniculus, a rabbit'. It also meant an underground passage, which is pretty understandable. And the Italians have stuck to their guns, because their word today isn't far different: 'coniglio'. So what the Hell is it with the French and their 'lapin'?

The Germans say 'Kaninchen' which is a small 'Kanin', whatever that was (it isn't in my dictionary at all). If it means 'canine', they've got it wrong, haven't they? In Spain, it's 'conejo', by the way. I wish I hadn't started this.

But I have to make it up to seven, now I've got this far. I am more happy than you know, to announce that it is 'Nokwatva' in Kaffir, and I hope that helps you as much as it does me because at last I can drive on, and drag my thoughts back to reality.

★★★

Once past Bicester it was too late to start looking for another phone-box; and glancing at my watch by the light of Bicester's final street-lamp, I saw surprisingly that I had still only been on the journey for two and a half hours, including two lubrications; so I decided to ring after I had got into Oxford. I turned off the main road, as I often did, towards the village of Islip, because this would cut out a tedious network of junctions, roundabouts and obstructions imposed by the local council and mis-described as 'traffic calming'. Calming be buggered, there can be few things more infuriating to the average born-calm motorist.

I was talking earlier about foreigners' difficulties with our placenames, and I quoted some well known examples; but all around me now were names that probably present a problem though to us they may look harmless at first sight. Yes, we all know about Bicester; but at Islip there is the River Cherwell, and how about that? Is Islip 'Is lip?' or 'I slip?'. "Into the river" is probably the best way to teach our visitors. And as for 'Cherwell', even some of the locals, and for Heaven's sake the folk on Radio Oxford, get it wrong. But while I criticise them, I have to confess that The Admirable Ekwall shows us two early Anglo-Saxon spellings, (always remembering that the 'c' was 'ch', and that these were being written down by a scribe who was listening to the local landowner): in AD 681 'Ceruelle'; but in AD 864 and many times thereafter 'Cearwell' or words literally to that effect, the 'a' having crept in.

I'm sorry to do this to you, but have you noticed those different pronunciations of the letter 'C'? In the above it was obviously said like out 'ch', as in modern Italian. A host of examples from our mutual friend indicate that the full 'ch' began to make its appearance in the eleventh or twelfth century, depending on the level of education and sophistication of the place, or of the visiting scribe. Charing in Kent began as 'Ciornincge' in 799, but was already 'Cherringe' by Domesday; and so was Chelsea given its 'h' in DB; whereas just across the moor from Islip, Charlton (Cerlentone in Domesday) only is

'Cherleton upon Ottemour' by 1314. Even today we have trouble internationally with the letter 'C'.

How did the Romans pronounce their Latin? When Julius Caesar bragged "Veni, Vidi, Vici" was the last word 'Vichi', 'Vissi' or 'Viki'? Nowadays I suspect it is still said in three different ways depending on where and who you are: by the Italians, by the old school teachers in our dustier public schools, and by the rest of us.

★★★

Islip is a pleasant unassuming village today, but it has greatness in the background, for this was the birthplace, at the end of the tenth century, of King Edward the Confessor: he who caused us such a load of trouble by the confusion after his rather inconsiderate death in 1066. Why was such an important Royal born in such a little place, I have often wondered when driving through, because he was born 'into the purple', by no means an upstart King. It has struck me, thinking it through, that most young women, when about to give birth, are inclined to go home to mother. I wonder whether Queen Emma, feeling that her time was coming, wanted the comfort of people around her whom she could trust? Edward's Dad, Aethelred, may have been Unready but I'm damn sure she wasn't...

Or maybe she actually was: sort of taken short, before the due time? After all, I see that the mother's name in full, as we have it, was Emma of Normandy. French lady, eh? Then what on earth was she doing, eight or nine months pregnant, in the moorland wilds of Oxfordshire? Was her mum living in the village?

We will never know, unless somebody finds a parchment written by a Saxon midwife (Middle English colloquial: 'middif') or the local priest, and the scroll filed away for posterity in Islip church tower. Call me, Vicar, if I can help.

When you have pondered all these weird possibilities, it is important not to let them take hold of you. The through road at Islip, after passing the church and a tableau of honey-brown Cotswold houses, dips down to the bridge over the gentle River Ray. This, in a couple of minutes, will flow into the Cherwell which lurks a stonesthrow away to your right, and then be carried off rather anonymously to join the all-powerful Thames in Oxford itself under Magdalen Bridge where, in my day long gone, punt-hire still wasn't much more per person, than "a groat for a boat"! But the Ray has a chance, once every year, to make its presence felt: it floods very easily, and at the foot of that dip in the road, you will find in Springtime a great deep pond submerging the area outside the bridge-side pub.

Given the right time of year, the right shade of darkness and the right moonlight glistening through it, Islip with its hushed old golden houses and sliding stream, evokes real memories of Queen Emma and her son and it can be a place full of ghosts.

But I have a theory about ghosts; this is it.

THE HAY MILL HAUNTINGS

An elderly chap in a dark blue suit was sitting all by himself on the riverbank in the middle of nowhere. This is what he told me.

Upstream from that lovely old town Ludlow, *(he said)* the unruly River Teme sweeps through shallows to a rocky gorge; and there, walking and exploring late one summer day when I was young, I emerged from the woods of the Chase to come suddenly upon a deserted tumbledown watermill, its wheel mossy and awry, much of the roof missing, and the rest of the place leaning as if wishing to dive into the torrent.

I say 'deserted'; but I then saw from the crooked stack of the chimney a thin line of smoke, ash-grey in the afternoon sun. My curiosity led me in. Heavy-beamed with the low ceiling one would expect, there was just the one liveable room. A wide inglenook glowed red; and before it, in a fluffy armchair, sat an aged man who, so far as I could tell in the haze, was in tatters, though he had round him a long and comforting red scarf, hand-knitted, so somebody must have loved him once.

He was smoking – and even now as I remember this, I can hardly believe it – a long clay pipe: yes, clay, as three hundred years ago. He turned to look, beckoned me into the room with it, and pointed to the kettle that hissed on the hob, then to a teapot and some cups on tie hearth. So far not a word had been said, but I sensed what was required of me. He then waved, still with the pipe, to a dark oak joint-stool across at the further side of the fire – decrepit but genuine, it would fetch a fortune today – and at last he spoke.

"The milk is in a billy-can hanging in the river. I go up to the farm once a week, very early, and make friends with a cow, but don't tell anybody." When I came back, he asked: "What is your name, young man?"

I told him. "Alan."

"I myself," he proclaimed with a slight touch of grandeur, "am Cornish, and my name is Hugo Horningtopps. It is a strange name and I suspect it has come to me from the pixies, don't you know." To him, this apparently explained everything, because he just puffed away while we both sipped our tea. But I was curious for more.

"Do you live in this place all the time?"

"I am a researcher, and I have found this the ideal place for my work." For the first time, looking around by the light of the flickering logs, I saw that the far end of the room was a wall of books, up to the rafters, old and dusty like some forgotten overflow from that other Hay, down on the Wye. "And," he added, "as a warning, I must tell you, Alan, that nobody will listen to me and everybody thinks I'm mad."

I began to chuckle at this but quickly saw he was serious. There was a perceptible note of distress in the voice, so I had the sense to change direction.

"That is what fools say about genius, isn't it? What is the nature of your 'madness'? What do you research?"

"The occult." He waved his pipe at the pile of books. "The mysteries of visitations. The ghosts that favour us with their appearances…"

No doubt he was well accustomed to the sort of

reaction I displayed: one smiles and shrugs, an eyebrow lifts, one's head tilts a little. But he just looked at me hard and confidentially.

"Oh yes. They do, my friend."

And there was something different now in the voice.

"I see them... Right here... All the time..."

What could I do but sip my tea, and encourage him to continue? I pulled the stool closer. I was due at the pub in Leintwardine, three miles further up the river, but not till late, and it was not yet evening. Acting out the obvious old cliché, we put another log on the fire.

* * *

"You see, Alan," he began, "some people – very few admittedly, – possess an extra – in my strange case extreme – sensitivity: we can somehow perceive happenings which are – how can I put it – outside the normal accepted range, as for instance dogs can hear sounds beyond the human ear, don't you know?"

Yes, I knew about this: he was talking some sense.

"So, as they have extra sound, you have extra vision?"

"It seems so," he nodded sadly. "I see things."

"But you said just now, you see ghosts – *all* the time?"

He explained that we were in a particularly receptive area for these apparitions: we all know, he said, that ghosts are most often encountered where tragic and bloodthirsty events are recorded; and he quoted the nearby battles of Ludford Bridge, of Mortimer's Cross, and to the West not only the massacre at Pilleth but the whole terror-torn Border, with Offa's Dyke "where my Welsh cousins would come swarming across." He picked from the floor a local Ordnance Survey map (and I noted that it was a very old edition, printed on cloth and ink-marked all over). He showed me that more than thirty ruined or earthworked castles were within a few miles of us, each one nursing its own grim secrets.

"Imagine," he said, folding it away, "the disappointments, the griefs, the accumulated agonies of all those people, over all the centuries. And sitting here, I see those people – they pass through, come and go…"

"Have you told this to anyone?"

He shook his head. "We don't like to, we who have this curse."

"Curse! But surely – ."

Suddenly he shushed and whispered: "There! Behind you!" I had that cold electric trickle up my spine; but I nervously swung around. There was nothing, just a puff of smoke out of the inglenook as I moved.

"Silly of me," he apologised. "Of course you wouldn't have seen him."

I asked what 'he' had been.

"Just a military man… Probably Tudor… An officer, this time, clothing like the pictures we see of Drake or Raleigh back from the Americas…"

"Did he have a clay pipe?" I asked flippantly, "or was he chewing gum?" Hugo looked at me sadly.

"You see, you all just joke. I can't prove anything to you but my researches are almost done. I only need to work out why it is just here, on this spot, that I see them."

But soon it was no longer a matter of indulging an old mad man. Despite myself, I was impressed by his arguments; as it grew darker, I went on listening, increasingly enthralled, as with an occasional "Hush – There!" he recounted one 'sighting' after another.

These were mostly the shades of ordinary people, who must have met their unhappy end in those parts, and he saw them as they moved towards, or more likely fled, the sites where their troubled bodies lay. Their dress could usually place them in a certain century. A few were apparently Roman, he said, because there had been a major frontier town where little Leintwardine now sat beside its two rivers.

Mention of the village brought me, startled, back to reality, I was late. I assured old Hugo that I believed him: I told him he had not a curse but an incredible gift. I bade him Farewell and hastened along the riverbank, over the Rainbow Bridge and on to the pub. It was close to midnight and I had to rouse the disgruntled landlord.

***

I came down blearily to a late, cold and fatty breakfast, and to scowls from the kitchen. There was a letter for me: in a re-used envelope and just marked "Alan", it was written in an elderly script, on endpages torn from some yellowing book. It has changed my life…

My Dear Friend

Indeed, my only friend…

Our unexpected meeting in yesterday's twilight was surely predestined? For you have given me the final key I was seeking. I now know the truth about ghosts, and can move on. Because I know no-one else, and because of your vital contribution and kind understanding, I appoint you to be custodian of my secret.

But I must also impose on you. The news must be released in my own name, in which – in its uniqueness – I take pride. And as for the forename, always my unfulfilled wish, had I been blessed with a son – 'Timothy'; that Timothy whom Saint Paul so wisely advised not to "give heed to fables".

So, my Timothy, I can tell you: *Ghosts Are Real.*

The visitors I have seen at Hay Mill, and I believe all such apparitions, are indeed passing through: we have just misread one thing – their direction.

You see, the one great barrier we still have to overcome is Time: and this, one day, we will do. But as soon as that mystery is solved, there will be an all-too-human commercialisation of it! It will be exploited like Space Travel will be, just as nowadays we cruise the ruins of the Mediterranean.

Alan – Timothy – we are seeing Time Travellers, but from the future. Dressed according to the century they plan to visit, which is obvious, we see them fleetingly as they go back in Time. And tourists being what they are, it can be hopelessly mundane: no doubt some jovial excursionists enjoy walking around the White Tower with their 'head' under their arm, do you think? (I have worked it out all night but still have to ponder the headless horseman of Caxton Gibbet – this one I bequeath to you).

But, dear boy, most banal of all is the vital clue you so splendidly gave me, last evening. It suddenly came to me: that Tudor officer was not just speaking as he went past us (I can see them but never hear them); God help us, he really *was* chewing gum! Evidently our tourist industry will live on!

And why have I been seeing so much of this traffic? I think future times will bring great hosts of such visitors, and I guess the flow will have to be closely controlled, with a system of 'disembarkation points' perhaps? The site of Hay Mill must be one: who knows how today's fields might develop in days to come. And then, rivers last forever – perhaps they come up the Teme until the shallows?

One day, we will all know. But for me, I want to find out, now. I suspect that recent arrivals into the future have to delay a return — you never hear of recent ghosts, do you? So, dear boy, here is my promise...

I will return, in fifty years, and do my utmost then to make contact with you, where we met. There will be much to talk about. Precisely fifty years, to the day.

Au revoir. H.H.

I folded the letter away. My coffee was as cold as the bacon and eggs, and I went to pay the bill. There was a small crowd in the foyer, and a wet red scarf in somebody's hand. An old vagrant, they said, had been found in the river.

And that is why, tired and grey after fifty years, I sit here on the riverbank by the swirling Teme. The mill has gone: no doubt, for failing to conform, neither healthy nor safe.

Or, was it ever here? Did I imagine old Hugo?

But then, there had been the scarf…

Well, anyway, I am keeping the appointment. Fifty years to the day, I am here. He will come soon.

I have done my duty, passed on his discovery and his name.

But very soon now, he will come.

But if not, old and alone as I am *(said the man in the suit)* – then I, Tim Topps, will go and join him.

When I got as far as the Rainbow Bridge,
I looked back to the riverbank. There was nobody.

VIII

The road to the Onions

Once over the bridge and up the hill out of Islip, and leaving behind its ghosts – whichever direction they come from – I was briefly back with the Romans. Across to the left, if it had been daylight, I would have caught a glimpse of the spread tablecloth that is Otmoor: the network of square-hedged fields which, one is told at the pubs, gave Lewis Carroll his chessboard idea for the Looking-glass book. And slicing across the moor is the Roman road from Dorchester-on-Thames. Moreover, as I turned right towards Oxford, a small wood is said on the map to mark the site of a Roman Temple…

Or at least, it used to. On the latest editions, it has been omitted and I would love to know why? Was it a mistake? Has it all been dug up and filched away? Or did the farmer get fed up with people trampling his crops with their metal-detectors? Maybe he himself is bleeping about?

In any case, I have always thought it a rather unlikely place for a Temple: so far as I can see, there are no sacred springs around; and it's far away from the old road. Perhaps some Victorian antiquary from the University had a bit too much imagination? And now, I see, they have for the first time marked a Roman Villa, no less, a couple of miles back towards Islip. What is going on?

★★★

I was getting hungry and was happy to know that a meal would be awaiting me, very soon. My thoughts naturally drifted back to the Roman diet. Given that today's Italians are pasta-and-tomatoes personified, whatever did they do in the Middle Ages, before (as we are told) Vasco da Gama or one of that crowd brought noodles back from China, and Columbus or Raleigh or somebody found tomatoes in the Americas?

And another thing: haven't you silently doffed your hat to whoever it was that first discovered a tomato was safe to eat? I mean: look at it!

I think they must have eaten rice in the early days. I remember a film in the late forties, with a very well-built young woman standing in a paddy-field, defiant about something I can't recall in the least. It was in the South, that overly laidback part I have named 'Italian Domaniland'. I wrote to tell that joke to a paper, but you know…

Nowadays, of course, pasta must be one of their most important industries, and one has to admire their ingenuity in continuing to keep it so interesting because, after all, it's only a lump of dough when it starts. Not only are there special local shapes and sizes, but the names are so enticing: little worms, butterflies, pen-nibs, hair, and all the –ettis and –inos and –ones.

Another time I wrote uselessly to the papers was when I read about the deprivations suffered by the Italians in the war, when they were under the malevolent eyes of their German allies. A biography of Sophia Loren, growing up in Naples (where else?), tells that food was so scarce, and money in her family so lacking, she was driven to steal pasta from a local shop. "Penne-pinching", I suggested, but did they print it?

Theirs is such a lovely language, like velvet on the tongue; and with quite easy rules, too. I took a month's leave some years ago, to study Italian at the British Institute in Florence, a memorable four weeks, not least for the fact that our class consisted of middle-aged me and nine English sixth-form girls... Oh yes, and there was the Art and the Architecture, I nearly forgot. One of the girls, Sharon, was very bright and also very dishy, and furious at being perpetually ogled and harassed by swarthy males on the streets and in restaurants, not least by the waiters. Our teacher himself was quite young and clearly enjoyed his job: to me, he hardly spoke. However, he was telling us one day about all those adjectival endings to their nouns: the suffixes like -ino (little), -one (large), and then he got on to the more esoteric ones, like –accio (ugly so that Boccaccio is 'ugly mouth'); then he gave us '...' meaning a feeble man.

"Jesus!" said Sharon. "Italian men are so feeble they have to have a word for it!"

* * *

My thoughts were still, in those last few minutes as I headed into Oxford, centred around food: I knew that I would soon be focussing happily on a steaming plate of spaghetti carbonara…

Now that is a word we all understand these days, though it would have rung few bells in an average English assembly fifty years ago. It has become not just 'fashionable' but imperative, today, to include at the back of every glossy weekend magazine – tucked unavoidably into your heavy doorstep of a newspaper – page after page of cookery; every TV channel is knee-deep in chefs with their long hair dangling into the food, and their breath all over it.

What intrigues and irritates me is the grimly determined trend to be aggressively upmarket. It's only food, for God's sake. There are two clear lines of attack upon us native, well-meaning consumers of sausage-and-mash, fish-and-chips, or meat-and-two-veg, with the accompanying slur that we don't know how to cook sprouts.

The first assault is to suggest that all those perfectly-good dishes need to be 'improved' by adding a long list of ingredients, spices or exotic embellishments. Why? First: it is intrusive on our home cooking happiness, and it demands that we go out and buy a basket-full of incidental additives, the residue of which will then rot away or languish on the top shelf for years; and second, we have all tried such mixtures in the past few centuries and found for ourselves the small number that do actually work… We know that sausages-and-marmalade is good, and so is gammon-and-pineapple; but kippers-and-custard isn't.

The second attack on the English housewife is more subtle: it is designed to make us feel inept: uninformed about the finer side of cookery and thus useless in our kitchen. The method is a simple one, well-known both to the teachers at Stephen Potter's Yeovil and – rather less pleasantly – to Doctor Goebbels: blind them with unfamiliar science. I looked last week at the cookery pages of those shiny magazines, and noted down some of the recipe name-dropping. Some on my list will doubtless be known to many people; but surely others of them will be a crushing bewilderment to many more readers than just me: we have *barfi*, *brandade*, *cromesqui*, *galettes*, *girolles*, *labneh*, *manchego*, *mandoline*, *membrillo*, *passata*, *pursiane*, *remoulade*, *rillettes*, *rotolo*, *tagine*, *ventreche*, *voignier*… All on one day. OK, so I'm a peasant, but even peasants are interested in ways to cook food. Get yourselves down to earth and stop showing off. You are only cooks.

And stop making silly designs on the plates, instead of actually putting food on them – if I want to see Art I'll go to a gallery. From you, you conceited duffer, we just want easy and interesting hints on what to eat, economically and healthily.

I felt much better now, looking forward to my pasta tonight and perhaps liver-and-bacon at the Mitre tomorrow? Yes, and thick onion gravy, too, made the old fashioned way. Don't draw pictures on my plate with it. Oh, and some English mustard, yes English. And a bottle of house red. Whatever's cheapest, I'm not here to impress you.

★★★

The little hamlet of Woodeaton sits on the first bend in my road, and I have sometimes stopped at its tiny church just to look at the pews. I have done the same at the equally small village of Hauxton, near the Shelfords outside Cambridge. The experts on ancient oak are always enthusing about the usual over-decorated masterpieces, but I find a much greater and more deeply romantic appeal in the work done, back in the Middle Ages, by the local village carpenter who had the oaktree cut down and sliced into a manageable set of planks, from which he would devotedly create these primitive benches for his friends in the local congregation. There is something very moving, when you stroke the old hand-weathered timber and try to imagine the people of the time. The same applies to other types of what the sniffy dealers and auction-boys dismiss as being just 'country furniture'. But, believe me, your 'country' oak sideboard for which they will give you a few hundred and claim to be doing you a favour, will later appear in a West End showroom marked at a couple of thousand. How come? Oh well, you see, a lot of restoration was needed, unseen to the untrained eye; and of course, there was no real provenance; and oh, yes, storage while all the work was going on; and then the charge made by the oak expert who examined the piece prior to display. (Oh yes, and our rent and our insurances and my salary). And of course, you know, it was only 'country'.

Halfway, now, to the suburb of Headington, where there are quarries which supplied most of the honey-coloured stone for the Oxford Colleges. But before that, a further mile of narrow road between arable fields; and parked beside the road, a complicated agricultural machine… Back again went my drowsy memory…

This is a rural, farming community, and you would expect it to be self-contained and resistant to the malign influences of the outside world; but I had just driven past this huge agricultural machine, which, at a moment's notice, sparked off in me all the latent memories I have of that wonderful man, Alfred Hitchcock.

Yes, he was sucked in by Hollywood; but his great achievement was his resistance to them and his determination to stay English. Right through his career, his jokes remained Englishly subtle. In 'The Trouble With Harry', I think his only outright comedy, the elderly retired sailor, Captain Wiles (Edmund Gwenn) is being entertained supremely innocently to tea by the also elderly Miss Graveley (the wonderful Mildred Natwick). They are being delicately polite to each other. She has just said that her dear father has passed away.

"I trust he had a peaceful end?"

"He was dragged into a threshing machine."

All done completely dead-pan. Later, Edmund Gwenn catches sight of the nubile young Shirley McLaine (in her first film) and rather delightfully says to a friend: "I wish I was 18 months younger." Again the English touch.

⋆⋆⋆

We – or certainly the Americans – seem to have lost irretrievably the art of making quiet but really brilliant films, that glory in the tight script and the smooth acting, without all these useless excesses of explosions, machine-gunning and other spectacles which – if they excite at all – occupy the mind for just a passing second and don't do it much good. What has gone wrong?

I suspect that the people at the top in today's cinema, are also in control of the preservation or demolition of the past. All these 'remakes' which nearly always fail to match up to their originals, and are cluttered up with non-entities, become flops despite all their efforts to promote them.

Let us thank God for all the off-beat TV channels which still allow us to make our own minds up, and rejoice in the memory of the brilliance of Billy Wilder and his deserving successor Neil Simon.

There are subtleties in all their films which, I'm sure, trace back to us in England, although we have to admit the welcome addition of the Jewish self-deprecating humour, which adds a savour all its own. (In that ridiculously funny spoof of the Western by Mel Brooks, we have an irate resident of a benighted cowboy town seeking revenge upon the raiders. They are suggesting ways to get their revenge. One suggestion: "Let's kill all their firstborn!"… "No, too Jewish.") Now, that's funny.

One has to admit: the funniest jokes are the non-politically-correct ones. PC, and the overwhelming humourlessness of our bureaucratic lords and masters, carries within itself a sort of Governmentally-approved poison: kill all wit, in case it is anti-establishment. It's not, with us, that bad yet: but is it coming?

That is the way regimes fall.

★ ★ ★

As soon as I started thinking about the ways to imprison or execute the politically-correct, while driving up to the Headington roundabout, my thoughts returned to my awful family, and to prisons in particular. If I turned left at this point, it oddly occurred to me, I would come to Wheatley, and there, standing mysteriously in the centre of the village, is a weird conical building in brick, with a door in it. Many visitors (OK then, a few of those passing through) assume it must be some sort of storage-place for the council road-sweepers; I enjoy correcting them. It was the lock up. I have dreamt of putting my brother-in-law in it...

I was on the last lap now. Straight through Headington, stopping only at the pathetic range of pedestrian-friendly traffic-lights outside Oxford Brookes University, relentlessly red at all unlikely hours, just in case one of their students is so unutterably stupid as to wander across the road with his (her?) eyes shut.

But then comes Headington Hill; and an incident from long ago.

JUST THE ONIONS

"Just the onions," his wife called after him that morning, as he cycled away to College from their caravan. "Please don't forget this time... And don't be late back, I need them for the hot-pot..."

So here he was at teatime, heaving back up the hill with his bike-basket full of books from the library, and an economics essay to complete by morning, and a pound of onions wobbling on top of it all… Behind him, relaxing in the students' common room before sauntering into Hall for their evening meal, were his unmarried colleagues who might, after Dinner, gather in twos or threes for a couple of hours' stimulating talk before retiring to their atmospheric oak-panelled rooms, to work and smoke and drink and dream… While he carried sodding onions uphill to a suburban sodding caravan park.

But still – . With an effort he cut short his envious thoughts. He had plenty of advantages they didn't have. For one thing he had a sense of proportion and of responsibility… a level-headed attitude… He had made a flying start into adult life, and without doubt he was a much more mature young man, better able to organize his work, get down to the real nitty-gritty of studying, which a University course was all about. After all, he'd done everything in the right order: after getting his Scholarship, he'd had two years of National Service – an education in itself. Now he was all ready for the future. Some of those others were still elongated children: you could tell an ex-service freshman from a third-year finalist who'd come straight on from school, everyone said so… More mature, definitely, he repeated to the topmost onion, which grinned back at him.

Yet only the other day, his tutor had said an odd thing. "Yes Peter," he'd said through the usual clouds of pipe-smoke, "the essay's O.K., the presentation's fine, you've got all the points in there… But do you think perhaps it's – don't you know – even a bit *too* good? I wonder if it's so solidly good and intense that you can't see through the facts to the real world beyond... What clubs and societies do you belong to here? Do you get out and play much sport, or..." He had embarrassed himself and spent a long time knocking out the pipe; then went on: "You're here to put some all-round finishing touches to your education, not just to grow perfect in one direction, don't you know? More three-dimensional I'd like you to be, even if more roughly-sculptured."

He got off the bike and brooded about that, up the steep hill out of town. What a lot of nonsense it all was.. What did these ivory-tower dons and these flippant well-heeled ex-schoolboys know about real life and normal living? Of course he used to have varied interests – music, history, archaeology – but now he was a grown-up married man, sharing with a loving young wife the excitements and day-by-day wonders of... of... worrying where next month's rent for the van was coming from. Of how on earth to make ends meet during the vacations... Not for them a cosy parental home to scurry back to... What he had was real living, real character-forming, and at the end of the day he'd... He'd cycle home to bloody hot-pot, he ended furiously.

Feeling suddenly overwhelmed with a tightness welling up in his throat, he vented his anger on the bike as he pushed it; not quite kicking it but shaking the handle-bars; and the topmost onion jumped from its brown bag and began rolling down the hill.

Hell, he thought. As he watched it bouncing away, this little triviality seemed the last straw, a sort of symbol of his utter uselessness... of the futility of what he was making of his life. Several times recently, he now confessed to himself, he had wanted desperately to break away, escape from everything: chuck the course, chuck the scholarship, chuck the van, chuck the wife, and-.

Did he mean that? It was most unfair, she had done nothing wrong, not a thing wrong except to let herself be talked into marrying the wrong man... or the right man too soon... or what it was. But yes – he *did*. He did mean it. He wanted longingly, *longingly* to run away. He leaned against the roadside wall and shut his eyes, trying for quite a long time to control himself...

★ ★ ★

A girl's voice said soothingly: "There, there, it's only an onion." He looked, and saw a tangle of sun-blonde hair, a smiling mouth and a couple of amused brown eyes. Between them and his face, a hand was holding his runaway vegetable. "Don't take on so," she said, "That which was lost is found."

She, also, was pushing a bike up the hill: neither a shopping bike of the orthodox sit-up-and-beg design, nor a racer where you saw nothing but tarmac as you crossed the landscape – this was what he would describe as stylish but efficient. She, he thought, was probably the same.

He thanked her, and she returned the onion to its bag. "Snatched from certain death under that bus," she told him. "I reckon I deserve a medal." She peered into the basket. "Dear dear," she muttered, shaking her head sadly so that the hair fell all over the place, "a very nasty meal you're cooking up there – Economic Soup with a thin Philosophy Sauce. I should choke on that... Nearly did."

"Which college are you?" he asked.

"No College," she replied, "just passing through. I did a year's Economics at School... But it sort of gave me up." She nodded up the hill. "Are you going my way?"

They walked up side-by-side when the traffic allowed; and when it didn't, he took in more details of the slender figure and the pink jeans, the rucksack on her back and the two panniers by the rear wheel. She had decided to take a year off after leaving school and was just starting out on a cycling exploration of the Continent.

"Never could go before – well, you must be the same – what with the War and then all the austerity and not allowed any foreign money... We never really had any holidays when I was growing up; did you? But at least you've had a bit of a break, getting away on National Service – ."

He asked how she knew that. You can tell, she replied... and that made him feel better.

"Did you enjoy being marched off to all those exotic places? My brother was in the Far East, then Cairo..."

He laughed. "I savoured all the delights of the fairy town of Wolverhampton."

"I hope the natives were friendly?"

"Saturday nights they got a bit dangerous. But my two years were tantalizing – we had to issue stores to Army units all round the world, and it's a bit thick to sit on the industrial borders of Shropshire sending letters and parcels to Hong Kong, Panama, the Himalayan foothills and God knows where..."

"Poor old you," she said, "the only foothill you had was the Wrekin..."

"We used to drive out and sit looking at it," he recalled. "The locals say that if you can see it from a distance, it's going to rain; and if you can't, it's raining already."

"How are you on Roman remains?" she asked him, surprisingly.

"Ah yes, Wroxeter, just down the road that was: the ruins of Viriconium. I often went there, and a couple of times I met the chap in charge of the excavations... How do you know about that?"

"Just one of my things – I love visiting old places. That's what I'm going to do on this trip of mine. Look." She stopped, and reached into one of the panniers, to pull out a somewhat tattered map of Europe. "Let me show you."

They put their bikes against a tree and sat down on the grass. She spread out the map.

"I'm going across to Brittany – here – to see that marvellous prehistoric stone circle –"

"Wait!" He gave a gasp. Quite clearly at the bottom, the map read: Bartholomew 1866. "This map's completely out-of-date."

She opened her eyes wide and looked at him

innocently. "Oh dear, do you think the stone circle has emigrated?"

"No, but really – I mean – all the countries are different. This was even before the Franco-Prussian War. Look, you've got the Austrian Empire here, that was the Hapsburgs…"

"Ah, but I'm not going that way. Besides, *I* don't mind one little bit where all the countries start and finish, I'm not going there to see today, I'm going to see yesterday. All the old towns and places I want to find, they were there long before my Grandma's map… Anyway, I grew up looking at this old map, I love it."

"But the roads – ."

"Who wants to ride along modern roads with all the exhaust and clatter and the lorry-drivers whistling at you? Country lanes will do – I'm in no hurry – and Roman roads when there is one: they're easy to spot on any map."

He chuckled: "You're crazy, you know that?"

"Probably." She nodded: "But haven't we proved recently the whole world's crazy in one way or another – I prefer my kind… Don't you think we ought to see what mankind has achieved before we get too clever and blow it all up, and ourselves with it?"

"Those who can," he replied grumpily, "those who can afford it."

"Afford what?" she cried. Evidently she had fought off that objection before, doubtless with her family. "Cycling is free… I've got a tent, so no hotel or bed-and-breakfast unless I have an emergency or simply want to pamper myself… Food is food wherever you are, and the best food is the cheapest anyway… I'm only allowed to take fifty pounds out of the country, but I may well bring it all back again, especially if I can earn a bit by fruit-picking for a few weeks in the South of France."

"It's the sort of thing I've dreamt of all my life," he said, "especially in Wolverhampton."

She caught the wistful look in his eye. "Everyone's doing it," she encouraged him. "I'm meeting up with lots of friends over there, at one place or another… And think of the sunshine," she added. "Doesn't your term end soon?"

He suddenly realised he had not mentioned that he was married; nor, for that matter, anything else about his situation. Mad thoughts had been building up inside his head; but now the deep gloom which had hit him, back there down the hill, came flooding in again; yet he couldn't show it. "I've got a lot of things keeping me here," he said – and that was the truth, God alone knew!

"Pah!" she said, as they went back to their bikes. "Live a bit. I know what – you could ride around selling onions!"

Hell, the onions!… the hot-pot!… the essay!… Hell.

"For all you know," the girl went on, "by *next* Summer the Russians and the Yanks will have blasted it all away. The aqueduct at Nimes… The Alhambra… The Roman Forum… See them while you can."

"Get thee behind me," he said with a smile, but inside him it wasn't funny, it wasn't funny at all. He thought of the names on that old map… He saw a landscape of chateaux… of palazzos… of minarets. Venice, he thought: "I stood in Venice, on the Bridge of Sighs"… The Alps: Hannibal, crossing the Alps…

"Take the plunge," she said.

Caesar crossing the Rubicon… Athens… Istanbul, that used to be Constantinople, that used to be Byzantium…

"…Byzantium…" he said dreamily, out loud.

"Yes," she said softly. "And Samarkand." She quoted the poem: "I take the Golden Road to Samarkand…"

"No no," he broke in without thinking, "it's 'we'… In the chorus it's "*We* take the Golden Road – ." Then he stopped.

"Yes," she said again; and then in a practical voice: "Well, do we?"

He couldn't speak, just spread out his hands helplessly.

"Listen," said the girl, mounting her bike, "I'm stopping off at the Crown to meet a friend. I shall be pushing on at about seven – if you like you can check with me then." A quick smile, and she touched his hand. "Come and help me find the Golden Road," she said; and then he stood and watched as the lithe body in the pink jeans pedalled away and round the corner.

⋆⋆⋆

Back at the caravan he handed over the brown paper bag, and sat silently at the far table, his books open but all their words a pointless jumble… His wife was prattling away as she prepared the supper.

"Mrs. Adams says she thinks I look much better now… I'm sorry I've had to ask you to do all that shopping, but truly I wasn't feeling well…"

Byzantium... Samarkand... Quinquereme of Nineveh...

"...So I thought I'd go and see the Doctor again... So I went today, Peter..."

Golden Road... Yellow-Brick Road... Lonesome Road... Asphalt Jungle... Does the road wind upwards all the way?

What was she saying? "...And Peter, we'll have to move by then because, well darling, we can't possibly get a cot into this little van, let alone a playpen..."

Upward all the way? He remembered the next dreadful line: "Yes, to the very end." Across the caravan park, the church clock was striking seven.

"Why darling," his wife looked at him with concern, "what is it? Your eyes are all wet... Oh, don't say I've upset you..."

He shook his head, and smiled.

"No my love," he said. "No no, of course you haven't. It's just the onions."

IX

The end of the Bunny Run

I parked as usual outside the little flat I have long been sharing, when in Oxford, though of course I still continued to claim overnight hotel expenses – well, don't we all? My friend was wearing those sexy pink jeans I've always loved so much.

"Ciao. Is it over?" she asked as she kissed me, and handed me a whisky "I'll take the coat and Good Heavens, the gloves."

"Yes," I replied with a long-delayed sigh of relief. "All over."

Then I thought: "I must telephone." I had another drink and rang home.

★★★

It wasn't my criminal brother-in-law who answered, but a Police Inspector. It seemed they were already onto him. I told him who I was, and at once he became suitably deferential; also a bit embarrassed, I thought. "I'm terribly sorry to be the one to tell you," he said, "but I'm afraid your wife is dead."

"Dead?" (Dead, dead, dead, dead, dead, dead, dead!)

"I'm afraid so. She has been attacked viciously with a knife from your kitchen. We are holding her brother, who is well-known to us, and has a long history of violence, as you may know."

"Well, I don't really get involved with – ."

"Of course not, Sir, this must be very upsetting for you. But this brother has only recently been released and apparently there has been a family dispute over inheritance, so it all seems pretty cut and dried."

"There were terrible arguments between them," I agreed, "but why did he – ."

"We don't know, Sir, but apparently he gained access late last night through a window – ."

"A window! Really ? Good heavens."

"And he claims," said the Inspector, "that as he climbed in, he knocked something on to the floor in the dark, and when he picked it up, it turned out to be the kitchen knife all covered in blood – ."

"Good Lord."

"But we've done tests, and apart from your wife's – er, late wife's –"

(Late, late, late, late, late, late, late..!)

" – the only prints on the knife are her brother's."

I looked across the room, where my pink-denim girl had already put the gloves on the fire. The inspector was still talking… That lovely inspector… Yes, of course I realised I'd have to come back straight away. In the morning. Would it take me perhaps three hours, the journey? Only two, I corrected him.

"I have to warn you, Sir," he went on, "we must ask you to identify the body. It will not be a happy task for you, so we will come with you."

"Of course, Inspector." How nice of him to be so considerate. "I'll be there."

"And," he added hesitantly, "it won't be pleasant…"

Dead diddy dead dead.

"… she was stabbed five or six times."

But I have this wretched little habit.

"Seven," I said.

AFTERTHOUGHTS

Over a pint (which *I* had bought, come to think of it) a friend suggested that some – no, he said 'many' – of my stories could do with improvement, or "development"… How kind, I thought.

But then, why not? Some written long ago, others frankly dashed off to a deadline for an army newspaper I had surprisingly found myself editing during National Service, I had to agree. And after all, as I've written elsewhere, I have always had a slight gift for making a virtue of a necessity (strongly recommended!).

I am merely a poor shadow of people like the great O. Henry, or Saki (look him up, he wrote like a dream). So correct and improve me, by all means. Here are a few suggestions, but help yourself:

1. Lone Tree (p. 13). This, referring to the 1930s, may today be seen to have a slight tinge of "colonialism", though it flowed from my pen quite happily. The boys' dialogue with the taxi driver was perfectly OK for that time, just a gentle tease for the man they knew well, a good friend in fact. Should that sequence be re-written to satisfy today's more pernickety reader?

2. Lloyd George, etc. (p. 29). Long after I gave it a title, I added the somewhat truculent 'Anyway'. I quite like it, but can't describe why. Does it add anything? But never mind that: suppose, just after I'd left, my old mother had written to my younger sister. Would her letter have started: "My dear, there is something from my past that I need to tell you…", or: "Your idiot brother was here today…"? And if dear old Miss Wetherall had overheard our conversation, what would she have reported to her gin-soaked friends around the Scrabble table?

3. Status (p. 50). I wonder how the German girl would have reported these events? Or indeed that young African woman? (Mussolini's Italian Army had recently invaded the countries lining Kenya's Northern border, keen to match the huge victories of Hitler, so it was indeed a perilous time.)

4. Clear Blue Sky (p. 69). What might Angela have confided to her diary (and I'll bet she had one), first, as soon as he'd cycled away; and second, when she realised that *both* little wheels had gone? (If she – or her grandchildren – should read this, maybe one day I'll know.)

5. Mr Hertzog (p. 93). There's a big fault in this story and I wonder whether you spotted it? As it stands, the boy is a cheat, knowingly flogging fake autographs at school. His realisation of the truth should only come

after he has sold them; maybe meeting up with the Purser on a later voyage? I'll have to re-write this, unless of course you do...

6. Lesson One (p. 113). This is true from start to finish, as told to me by my Grandfather (many and many a time). But suppose it was made known, next day, to the Sergeant Major? Would he have sent a report to his Commanding Officer, criticising that old Corporal? Was the old man in the dubious habit of befriending young recruits? Or was the RSM himself inclined to be a "befriender"? In every simple story there lurk sinister (and potentially profitable!) undercurrents... (I never asked Grandad, of course – in fact, I've only just thought of it, times have sadly changed and I'm pretty sure he would have been horrified and locked me in the cupboard under the stairs again).

7. Hay Mill (p. 132). I'm not happy with this, it gets too bitty at the end. I've written about Hay Mill in other books because the place has a special meaning for me; but in my haste to rush the story off for a competition (where of course I came nowhere), I think I rather messed it up. The "story within a story" doesn't work well, I feel, but what do you think? Nevertheless, I'm quite proud of my theory about most ghosts coming from the future, and, whatever you do, retain the chewing-gum – it's the one clue essential to the story!

8. Just the Onions (p. 148). Another true story. I wonder

who she was, where she came from, where she was going and what she found over the next hill. Perhaps she has written about it? If not, someone should. And, oh, those pink jeans…

9. Finally (p. 158). Right at the end, not just on my last page, but after the very last line, there are two words I intended to add but then decided to leave to the imagination of the readers, thus crediting them with an intelligence which will make them happily close the book and recommend me to their erudite friends. Was this right?

(By the way, that last page is pure fiction – my real wives feature in my other books.)

Well, thank you for coming with me on the drive and I hope we meet again. Goodbye.